THE DEVIL I

The Devil in Her sees Doctor Alan Carter returning to England to stay with an old friend, Colonel Merton, after seven arduous years abroad — only to receive a terrible shock. He first encounters frightened locals who tell him tales of a ghostly woman in filmy white roaming the moors and slaughtering animals. Dismissing their warnings, he proceeds to Merton Lodge — and into a maze of mystery and death. While in *She Vamped a Strangler*, private detective Rodney Granger investigates a case of robbery and murder in the upper echelons of society.

NORMAN FIRTH

THE DEVIL IN HER

LINFORD
Leicester

First published in Great Britain

First Linford Edition
published 2017

A catalogue record for this book is available
from the British Library.

ISBN 978–1–4448–3238–9

Published by
F. A. Thorpe (Publishing)
Anstey, Leicestershire

Set by Words & Graphics Ltd.
Anstey, Leicestershire
Printed and bound in Great Britain by
T. J. International Ltd., Padstow, Cornwall

This book is printed on acid-free paper

Contents

The Devil in Her

1

Witch-Woman

It was a lovely setting for events so completely horrible.

The train clattered incessantly over the lines, changing rhythm momentarily at the points' crossings. Past the window whirled the green of spring fields, with early daffodils dancing in a light breeze which was rustling the early foliage of elms, oaks and yews.

It was as if everyone else in the world were dead, and I was moving along in a carriage that was drawn by no visible means. We began to cross a curve in the line, and with unreasonable haste I opened the window and pushed out my head to breathe the sweet hay-scent and the harsher, acrid fumes of the engine smoke. I saw the engine itself far round on the curve, and I could just make out the figures of the driver and stoker, toiling behind a curtain of hissing sparks.

I sank back, reassured. I knew what was wrong, of course. The specialist had told me that.

I'd been burning the candle at both ends.

A man can't work day and night, he had told me, in foreign climes where the temperature is at lowest ninety-five in the shade, without feeling the strain. When you begin to find you can't sleep, even for a few hours a day; when your eyes begin to go back on you, and images become hazy and ill-defined; when you have a moment's relaxation and your mind still labours on, chasing intangible, half-formed thoughts into the recesses of your memory and digging into the various aspects of your latest experiment — well, that's the first sign. Unless you lay off immediately, there probably won't be a second sign. Your brain will just go, and your brainstorm will arrive, with mercy knows what results.

I hadn't liked to leave the experiments. You don't when you're fighting cholera in China, and helping those poor illiterate peasants. They're so damned grateful for all you do that it embarrasses you. But I realised I wouldn't be much better off than they were if I went back and had the expected brainstorm. So I stayed in Hang-Kow, and then took the first boat back for England, home and peace.

I felt better. But I still had these moments of fear, as if something were sneaking up on me when I was alone.

That was why I had written to Colonel Merton and as good as thrust my society on him. I had told him I was in England, and I had omitted to mention my threatened breakdown. I had asked if I might stay at Merton Lodge for a few weeks.

His reply hadn't been very encouraging. That was odd, because I really was an old friend of the family. I had been brought up next door, next door being a quarter of a mile away, and had played with Colonel Merton's three children, Archie, April and June.

June! I wondered how she was, and if she had changed much since my mother had died, and my father and I had moved to London. She had been fifteen then. That meant she would be almost twenty-two now. In these past seven years I hadn't seen or heard from her, except a brief letter of condolence when my father had died shortly before I took my medical degrees and left for China.

It had been mainly my fault that we had not kept in touch. I never had been a clever letter-writer. I had let things slide, and I doubted if she even knew my address at Lin-Yutang.

But now she came back with a rush. Every memory of her that I had cherished through those seven years crowded into my mind and heart: her sleek hair; her fresh, healthy cheeks; her white, even teeth.

Yes, I suppose we had been childhood sweethearts. It seems so naïve, but actually it amounted to that. I recalled more personal things: love notes, that first wonderful kiss under the old elms in the grounds of the lodge, the two hearts and names carved for eternity, or almost eternity, on the bole of the great old oak near the lake.

I remembered so well her white, shimmering beauty on that last day. She had worn a simple tennis dress, and she, Archie, April and I had been playing doubles. Archie and April had gone into the lodge, and it was time for me to leave. June and

I had wandered through the grounds, laughing and smiling, joking about the good times I'd have in London.

'You will write, won't you, Alan? Promise me! I don't know how I'll be able to stand it here when you're gone.'

My arm went about her waist, and I whispered gently: 'I'll write, dear, and someday I'll come back to you.'

I hadn't written. Now I wished I had. But at least I was coming back to her ... if she had waited for me.

I was roused from my pleasant reverie by the sound of the train entering Pikeville station. I was sorry I had been so hasty, as I had neglected to let them know the time of my arrival. I'd just sent a brief wire stating 'expect me tomorrow' and nothing else.

I was soon to regret it more, as there was no available transport. The village lay quiet and still in the gathering dusk, and its tiny streets were devoid of life. I decided that before starting what was to be a lengthy walk to the lodge, I would like a drink to soothe my parched throat. I turned into the Jugged Hare, the local inn.

There were four or five men whom I did not know clustered around the bar. Their tankards of beer were in front of them, but the usual yokel-ish chatter and merriment was conspicuously absent. As I came through the door, they turned towards me, stared, then turned back to their drinks.

'Good evening,' I said cheerfully. 'A lovely day it's been, gentlemen. A glass of mixed, landlord, please.'

Not one man had replied to my greeting. Silent and dour, they continued to regard their beer stolidly, without extending me the courtesy of even a nod.

The landlord, surly and badly shaven, slopped a mild bitter into a glass and thumped it on the counter in front of me. I laid down a ten-shilling note and said: 'Perhaps you gentlemen would join me?'

They looked at me again, and it seemed I was being summed up. The oldest there, half his face covered by a mass of grey beard, suddenly started and peered at me keenly. 'Ay! Yur be Captain Carter's boy, young Alan, be yur not?'

'That's right,' I said, smiling and feeling better now that someone had remembered me. 'I'm afraid I can't quite place you.'

The mechanism went into operation again, and brought forth a further selection of dialect. 'I be Ben Salter, young feller. Like as not ye'll have furgotten me — but I remembers yur well, ye and them imps of Colonel Merton's. Allus up tur mischief, yur wus.'

Then I had to tell him where I had been and what had brought me back to my birthplace. I did so as briefly as possible, and when I had finished, he shook his grey head dubiously.

'This place be no good fur putting yur mind to rest, Mister Alan,' he grunted. 'Thur be strange things going orn.'

I was interested. Strange things? Could that be the reason for the surliness, the unusual silence of the place? I asked him.

'Might be Alf could tell yur better nor me,' he said, nodding to the landlord. 'Oi be biased, but 'e be fresh down from thur city. Happen he'll tell ye what he thinks on all this yur.'

The landlord set down his glass and looked at me, some of the surliness gone from his face. He said in a Cockney accent:

'Not 'alf! I'm getting out 'o this screwy place, mate, ruddy quick! The brewery sent me dahn 'ere, blarst 'em, but I don't give an 'ang if I loses me job. I told 'em as 'ow I wants a relief man, and soon as 'e comes, aht I goes!'

I couldn't understand all this and I said as much. Alf looked at the others, glanced furtively at the door, then lowered his voice. He said: 'It's 'ard ter explain, mister. But wot it amounts to is this: there's been a woman, all dressed in filmy stuff, seen galloping about the fields an' moors. There's been dogs fahnd wif their t'roats slit open — an' sheep, likewise.'

'It sounds incredible,' I said. 'What's the woman like? Who is she?'

'Nobody rightly knows,' droned old Ben. 'But they do say she be possessed, bewitched! There be nobody who'll get close enough to her to have a right look. They'm afeared o' the evil eye, that's what.'

'What?' I gasped.

'Ay, the evil eye, I says. Them witches have the evil eye. If they look at you, there's sickness an' death comes to you, an' this woman be a witch, what else? Why

10

would she kill hens and dogs and sheep, if it weren't fur blood sacrifices? We be all afeared on her ... even Bill Jerms, the police officer.'

Here was the old legend cropping up again in full force in Pikeville. Garnished with elaborate trimmings, too! A woman roamed the moors killing sheep, dogs, and poultry and drinking their blood. A woman in filmy white. A woman who was either a witch, or bewitched!

'Well,' I said, 'I'd better be starting off for Merton Lodge. Good night, gentlemen. I expect I'll see you around the village before I leave again, Ben.'

'Wait a minute, sur,' said Ben, grasping my arm tightly. 'Be ye planning to walk to Merton Lodge this night?'

'I am.'

'Ye can't go, sur. It be too dangerous. Ye stop with me fur the night. Since Liza died, we've plenty o' room. Thur be only Sally, my daughter. Stop with me, Mister Alan. Ye can't walk acrost the moor this late.'

'Sorry, Ben. Thanks all the same. But the Mertons are expecting me. Don't worry, I know how to handle witches. Good night.'

I pushed open the door and went out into the moonlit night, leaving them staring after me, open-mouthed. Even though I am not superstitious, I had the feeling that I was about to encounter something essentially evil.

2

Blood Sacrifice!

I began to pick my way down the crumbling soil of the hill when the moon burst fully from behind a cloud. Then I stopped dead, my eyes glued on the middle distance where a number of what looked like sheep lay in a small field.

The hair on my neck prickled and rose as I stared, and my hands clenched at my sides. My knees felt suddenly weak. They trembled violently.

Across that far field, rendered small by distance but quite clear in the bright moonlight, flitted the form of a woman in filmy, flowing draperies, which at that distance looked like a diaphanous nightgown.

I could distinguish little else. The moonbeams played queer tricks with her flowing hair, making it difficult to recognise the colour. Her face was a mere dot in the distance. As abruptly as she had come, she

13

vanished into the shadows of some stunted trees.

I rubbed my eyes and stared hard. I wondered if I really had seen anyone, or if the talk in the inn had preyed on my already weakened mind and caused hallucinations.

Then, on the night air, from the shelter of those trees, came a wild and piteous bleating. Two or three sheep broke from cover and skittered away in terror over the field. There was a further frightful bleat, almost a scream of pain and horror, and then the figure of the woman came gliding swiftly into the open again. She moved rapidly, and before the lapse of a minute she was out of my sight again, behind a knoll of ground. I could only stand there motionless, the icy grip of terror contracting around my heart.

It must have been minutes before I finally moved; and then a strong sense of curiosity dragged my reluctant feet down the hill towards the point at which I had seen the woman and heard the screams.

The lamb was a pitiful sight. It was still kicking and struggling futilely on the ground, its throat ripped open by some sharp instrument. I turned away, sickened and horrified. So the story I had heard was true! It wasn't just my overworked brain which had concocted the whole dreadful affair! But where was the woman now? Whence had she come? And who was she? Might she not still be lurking about, waiting to commit further atrocities? Might I not myself fall a victim? Those who lusted for blood preferred human to animal.

I can say quite frankly that for the remainder of the walk to the lodge, I was a much perturbed man. My eyes darted before me, exploring every patch of shadow. My fists were continually clenched; and once when I began to whistle to bolster up my flagging courage, I stopped abruptly, afraid I might draw attention to myself — the attention of the woman who craved blood.

The relief I felt when finally I reached the lodge grounds was terrific. I really felt I had escaped a most horrible death. The front of the house was in darkness, and a glance at my watch told me why; the time was eleven-thirty. I had been on the move for two hours since leaving the inn.

I pressed the doorbell and heard it ring within. There was a moment's pause. Then footsteps approached the door, bolts were drawn, and the door opened a crack.

'Who's that?' asked a gruff voice I knew well.

'Carter, Alan Carter, Colonel.'

The door opened wider. I went in. My hand was seized firmly and shaken vigorously.

'Gad!' boomed Colonel Merton. 'Damned glad to see you again, my boy, what? After all these years, b'jove. You're certainly looking fit. Nothing like a trip overseas to bring out the best in a man, what? Tests his resourcefulness, eh? I remember when I was in Bengal … But that'll keep. Come in, come in.'

He hustled me towards the library, then took my hat and coat and whisked them away. Next he poured out a stiff drink to warm me up.

'I didn't know what time you'd get here, b'gad,' he barked. 'Thought you weren't coming after all. I knew the last train was at nine, and I thought you'd missed it when you weren't here by ten.'

'I got lost on the moors.'

He eyed me curiously, then said: 'You

16

look a bit white about the gills, m'boy.'

I told him what I had heard at the inn and what I had seen on the moors. He knitted his brows and nodded, saying: 'Yes, damme, it's true enough. Though heaven alone knows who she is, and what. That's why I wasn't so keen on you coming down, m'boy. But I knew if I'd mentioned my reasons in my letter, you'd have laughed at them. That's why I didn't say anything.'

'I would indeed have laughed at them,' I told him. 'But now that I've seen the — the thing myself, I feel very far from humorous.'

'That's how we all feel,' he acknowledged. 'We all dread that soon something more horrible than the mutilation of animals will take place. But thank heavens you got here safely. The youngsters have gone to bed. They're going riding early in the morning. Archie wanted to wait up, but I persuaded him to turn in.'

I was hurt that June hadn't waited up for me. Had she forgotten all about our youthful flirtation?

'I fell asleep in my chair,' Colonel Merton went on. 'The bell woke me up. Good job you arrived, m'boy. I should have toddled off to bed myself shortly. I think you know everybody here. Derek Denham is coming down tomorrow for a few days. He's my daughter's fiancé. Strapping young fellow.'

I had been eating the sandwiches with which he had plied me, but now they seemed to stick in my throat because of the lump which had suddenly risen there. I gulped. 'Your — your daughter's fiancé?'

He glanced at me quizzically, and suddenly chuckled. 'Of course, I forgot you and June were rather, well, that way about one another, eh? Don't worry, my boy. He's April's fiancé, not June's. June is still unattached, if you want to try your luck.'

I smiled and tried to disclaim any special interest. He went on: 'By the way, I suppose you aren't married yet, eh?'

I shook my head. 'You don't get much time for marriage out in China, sir. To be frank, I'm looking forward to meeting June again.'

'I'm surprised she didn't wait up for you,' Colonel Merton said, puzzled. 'Gad, until a few weeks ago she couldn't talk of anyone else but you. At the oddest moments she starts speaking about you for no reason. But now, well, she seems worried. In fact, she's not been herself since this damned witch, or whatever it is, started prowling.'

'It'll be nice to see June,' I said, changing the subject quickly.

'For her, too,' agreed Merton. 'Matter of fact, I've been looking forward to your arrival. I thought perhaps you'd be able to buck her up. This thing is getting her down, y'know. I offered to let her go to London for a few weeks, but she refused. I can't think what's come over her. Tonight she was very strange. Tell you what, m'boy. Why wait until morning to see her?'

'I — I don't quite understand,' I stammered.

'I mean, why not slip up to see her now before you turn in? She often reads for long stretches in bed. There's a chance she'll be awake still. At least you could knock and see.'

'But — but she might not like the idea.'

'Nonsense! There's nothing Victorian about me or my daughters. Why, you're almost one of the family. Off you go. I'll show you her room.'

He swept me, protesting, from the

library, and up the stairs. We reached a door on the second floor, and he nodded by way of encouragement. I tapped on the panels tentatively. There was no answer.

I said: 'She must be asleep, Colonel.'

'Pah! She isn't, unless she's dozed off. There's a light showing under the door. Here, let me try.'

He pushed past me and hammered loudly on the door. 'June?'

'Is that you, Father?'

'It is. There's an old friend of yours here. I think you ought to see him tonight, don't you? Are you respectable, my girl?'

'Who — who is it, Father?' Her voice sounded tense and worried.

'Alan Carter.'

'Alan — oh! I — very well. Wait a minute.'

The colonel yawned widely and excused himself. He said: 'Lover's meetings always make me tired, m'boy. I'll push off to bed now, I think. You don't really need any protection from me, what?' The broad-minded colonel slapped my shoulder, shook my hand, and said; 'June will show you to your room, m'boy, after you've exchanged reminiscences. Good night.'

I waited self-consciously for the door to open. The colonel had hardly gone when I faced June again — June, from whom I had parted so miserably many years ago.

She had scarcely altered. She was still the golden-haired goddess I had often held in my arms. Her eyes lighted momentarily as she saw me. Then, as if she had drawn a mask across her face, she gave me an awkward smile and said: 'Hello, Alan. Please don't stand on ceremony. Come in.'

I did so, nervously. 'June, oh — it's wonderful to see you.'

She merely nodded. Then she sat on an armchair near the dying embers of the fire, and beckoned me to sit in the opposite one. I fumbled with my case, which I still carried, but did as she indicated. There was something strange here. I only knew I wanted to take her in my arms again and pick up things where we had left off so long ago. I had thought she would feel the same. It hadn't struck me that she could have changed — but she had. Her eyes were friendly, but nothing more. That they masked some deeper feeling I felt certain.

If this were so, she gave no sign of it. She said softly: 'It's nice to see you again, Alan. How have you been?'

'Oh, fine,' I replied, trying hard to be nonchalant. 'Just fine.'

'I was very sorry to hear about — your — your father. It must have been an awful blow.'

'It was — but time, the great healer … you know.'

'Yes,' she said. 'It alters things, doesn't it, Alan?'

'Does it?' I said, gripping the handle of my case hard.

'It does,' she told me with conviction. 'Really.'

'But June …' My urbanity was deserting me. 'I didn't think it would have any effect on us; on the way we felt about each other.'

Her eyes were downcast as she said: 'We were children then, Alan. After all, we haven't even written, have we? We're almost strangers.'

'I see. You hold the fact that I didn't write against me?'

'No, Alan, please don't think that. It's just that I've changed myself. I can't understand it. It isn't as though I've met anyone else. I'm still heart-free.'

'Then there's a chance for your old flame?'

'No, Alan, no chance at all. I'm sorry.' Her tone was flat and final like a slap in the face. As my eyes dropped miserably to the floor, I noticed a set of woman's footprints — damp marks on the carpet; and June's discarded shoes, also damp. She had been out … recently!

3

Suspicion!

I tore my eyes from the tell-tale dampness of those shoes and from the wet marks on the floor. Then I began to notice other things — the light raincoat thrown hastily across the foot of the bed; the hem of the flimsy nightgown June wore showing beneath the edge of her dressing gown. It seemed as if she had made me wait at the door in order to give her time to slip her shoes off and get out of her raincoat, which meant she had recently been out ... which, in turn, meant that she might be the witch of Pikeville! There were tell-tale marks under the eyes — dark shadows. Lines of worry furrowed her brow, and there was that in the eyes themselves which spoke of dread and foreboding.

It couldn't be, I told myself, savagely — not June! Surely she couldn't be the witch-woman who roamed those desolate moors and fields, seeking blood sacrifices under the pallid rays of a spring moon. I burst out suddenly: 'June if you're in trouble, remember, I'm a doctor. I'd understand!'

I was unprepared for her outburst. Her eyes became suddenly clouded with anger, and she jumped to her feet, screaming: 'Don't look at me like that! I can't bear it! It — it's hateful of you. No — don't touch me. Leave me. Get out of my room.'

I stood up, amazed at her strident tone. I stammered something futile about talking things over in the morning, and her eyes flashed anew. She said, her voice now breaking: 'Oh, God, can't you leave me alone? This is what I was afraid of — afraid you'd try to meddle.'

Even I have a limit to the thickness of my skin. This was it. I stalked towards the door with as much dignity as possible. Then I turned and began to say: 'If you ever change your mind —' But, catching her look, I coughed and went out, closing the door softly behind me.

How long I tossed and turned, thinking of witches and evil eyes and blood sacrifices,

I cannot recall. But the flush of dawn was sneaking into my window when I finally fell asleep.

It was a bright, sunny day when I staggered downstairs. The clock hands pointed to eleven, and I wandered into the morning room, where one of the Mertons' two pretty maids served me with kidneys and bacon, followed by fresh fruit. I ate a good meal, then enquired about the rest of the family.

'They've gone riding, sir,' the maid told me. 'And Colonel Merton has gone to the station in the car to meet Mr. Denham, Miss April's fiancé.'

'I see. What do you think of this — this trouble that's been happening in the neighbourhood?' I asked pleasantly.

Her eyes registered horror and her fingers began to pluck at her neat starched apron. 'You mean — the — the witch-woman, sir?' she whispered. I nodded, and she said in scared tones: 'I'm frightened out of my wits, sir. So is Cook. She's leaving if there's any more of it. She says we'll likely all be murdered in our beds, sir.'

She left the room, and I crossed to the open French windows and looked out at the peaceful garden and green, sloping fields. It was hard to believe that when night came, terror would steal again over the village and its surroundings, chilling the hearts of all who lived there.

★   ★   ★

The tall, dark man in the black cape had just turned from the rough road and was negotiating the garden towards the windows. He spotted me standing there, and paused in indecision. Then, apparently making up his mind, he approached me. I stood back and allowed him to enter the room.

'Good day,' he said. His voice was soft and pleasant to the ear. 'I was looking for Miss Merton.'

'I'm afraid Miss Merton is not in at the moment,' I began, then I stopped in amazement as he burst out angrily:

'No doubt she instructed you also to give me that message! But I intend to see her, sir. Do you hear? She cannot treat Calantini thus. I insist that you inform her of my presence, and say that I will remain here until she sees me!'

I stared at him in surprise. He was indeed a peculiar fellow, and his clothing was in keeping with his foreign accent. His black cape was lined with red silk. His dark trousers were close-fitting, stovepipe-style, and his patent-leather shoes glistened in the morning sunlight. His hat was a wide-brimmed affair such as I should have imagined was common in Italy. His face was lean, like that of a hawk, and he possessed a predatory nose like the beak of a vulture, yet he was not ugly. His eyes were glittering with untold fires. They bored into me, and I felt a strange compulsion in them.

Abruptly I pulled myself together and tore my own eyes from his embarrassing gaze. I said stiffly: 'I've already told you that Miss Merton is not at home. She made arrangements to go riding. If she left instructions that she does not desire to see you, I am sure her breach of etiquette is quite justified. Good day, sir!'

'Have a care,' he grated harshly. 'Have a care how you speak, my friend. Remember, I am Calantini.'

'You make it hard for anyone to forget the fact,' I said tersely.

He expanded like a turkey cock, strutted to the settee and sat down, as if bestowing some signal honour upon the recipient of his emaciated carcass. He then fixed me again with his eyes. 'Who are you?' he demanded.

'My name is Carter,' I told him. 'Alan Carter. I'm a guest here.'

'I am Calantini,' he said.

'So I gathered.'

'Hmm! You are not, then, this, this Derek Denham?'

'No. I believe the gentleman is arriving today. Have you any business with him?'

'None. I wished to see him; nothing more. I wished to see the fool for whom April Merton has rejected me. Me — Calantini!'

He did not seem worried about this confession of his rejection by April. Indeed, the inference he presumably placed upon it was that she was a fool ever to have preferred anyone to him — Calantini. My own views differed. I was becoming rattled.

I said: 'I am not so sure her choice wasn't a wise one, sir. If she has no wish to see you, I would advise you to leave at once before

29

you say too much. I might inform you that I am a great friend of the lady in question, and if you offer her any insults, I'd be only too delighted to give you a good hiding.'

'Do you threaten Calantini? Italy's most noted psychiatrist?'

Fortunately at that moment, the morning-room door opened and Archie bounced in, beaming all over his vacuous features. His gaze rested on me, and he whooped: 'What ho! Old Frog-Face himself, back from the Orient.'

Then he was upon me, flinging my arm vigorously back and forth and thumping me heartily on the spine, babbling how grand it was to see me again — 'Absolutely top hole, what?'

This performance concluded, his gaze suddenly rested on Calantini, and he became less exuberant. He said: 'Ha! The jolly old witch doctor.'

Calantini rose, snorting. 'I consider your remark in bad taste,' he grunted in his soft yet penetrating tone.

Archie shrugged. 'That's as may be, old son, but there it is. April doesn't want to see you. She's told you repeatedly. If you must go about making a cad of yourself, you can't blame her. Now suppose you scoot, old son? Or must Alan and I bung you out on your blessed back?'

For a second the gaunt Italian paused. Then, with a gruff snort, he strode into the garden again.

Archie sighed. 'Poor chap. He's absolutely crackers about that blighted sister of mine. You know what passionate blighters these Latins are.'

'He did seem rather insistent,' I agreed.

'I expect he would. He took your old home when the last tenant left. He was a neighbour, and Father extended the usual courtesy call to him, which he returned. But the moment he saw April, he never left off chasing her. She strung him along for a time, said he was amusing, but when he tried to propose to her she turned him down flat. It seems he got a bit offensive. Anyway, she refused to see him again. Just as well, too, because this Denham chap's coming down. He's her fiancé, you know.'

'There may be trouble if the two meet, eh?'

'Sure to be. But Derek can handle six of

Calantini; I daresay he's a clever chap. If we believe everything the silly ass has told us, there's none to touch him. He's a writer, too, y'know. Writes stuff on black magic and all that rot. I got one of his books and read it — frightful tripe. He tries to verify that witches and demons really exist. I can't say I blame April for not wanting someone like that for a husband. It would hardly be nice sharing the blessed honeymoon couch with his jolly old familiar, would it? I mean, the familiar might get too familiar, what? Ha, ha, ha!'

I gazed at him admiringly. 'Still the same old Archie.' I smiled. 'Still trying to be a funny man.'

The door opened again and April came in. She looked wonderful, as usual, and from a tousle-haired schoolgirl she had grown into a beautiful woman — sleek, dark and svelte.

'I say, Archie, didn't I see that fool Calantini just leaving? I must say I'm glad I missed him.' Then, as her eyes fell on me, April said, 'Alan! Alan, darling. How wonderful to see you.'

Before I knew exactly where I was,

April's arms were round my neck and her lips pressed against mine. Archie stood by, grinning at my bewildered expression.

'Don't let her upset you, Alan,' he said. 'She finished her education in one of those demure French convents, and that's how they turned her out. Emotional, you know. Or sophisticated, if you want to look at it from that angle. Fat-headed, anyway.'

'Oh, don't be such an ass, Archie,' April said, standing back and admiring me to my confusion. 'My, hasn't he grown? Handsome, too. I expected to see him boasting a pigtail after being in China so long. Hmm! Some man! If June wasn't so keen on him, I believe I'd set my own cap for him.'

'You'd set your cap for anything in trousers,' Archie said with a wide smile. 'Including Calantini.'

'He was fun for a time,' admitted April. 'Do you know, I envy June.'

'You needn't worry about June,' I said darkly. 'She didn't seem over-pleased to see me.'

'Didn't she? Oh, well, she's been funny lately, even with us. She'll probably snap out of it. Now sit down and tell us all about

China. It must have been exciting. Did you ever go hunting tigers?'

'There are no tigers in China,' I said.

'Oh, aren't there? What a pity. You must have been awfully annoyed. Didn't you do any hunting?'

'Quite a lot. I hunted a quick curative remedy for cholera. I spent sixteen out of every twenty-four hours doing that. I can assure you it was just as exciting as hunting tigers.'

June came into the room at that moment.

'Well,' said April gaily, 'we've got something just as exciting to hunt for down here. What do you think? A witch-woman!'

There was a sudden tension in the room, and June's riding whip clattered to the floor. I turned and met her white, strained face. She seemed to be on the verge of a faint.

4

Menace in the Night

There wasn't much conversation after that. June picked up her riding whip and excused herself. April gazed after her sadly and remarked she didn't know what had come over poor old June. Archie seemed uncomfortable. Eventually April left, and Archie turned to me.

'I say, Alan, don't you notice something rather strange about — well, about June? Did you see the way — the way she reacted when — when April mentioned the — the witch-woman?'

It was an uncomfortable question to ask one who had been a stranger to the family for seven years. But seemingly June's coolness hadn't affected Archie. He still regarded me as he had done seven years earlier and wanted my opinion as a staunch and loyal friend. I gave it frankly: 'I don't like it, Archie. Not a bit.'

'It's worrying me,' he explained. 'Perhaps you heard about dogs being attacked?'

'I believe I did hear some mention of it.'

'How much did you hear?'

'Very little — just that dogs had been found with their throats mutilated by a knife. Why?'

'They were *our* dogs,' he said slowly. 'Don't you think that's strange?'

'In what way?'

'They were mastiffs — two of them. We kept them in separate kennels, chained up, one at each side of the yard. The guv'nor found out they'd been drugged before they were murdered.'

'Drugged?'

'Just that — with some quick-acting stuff. It's my idea that whoever did the job stole up on them, offered them some drugged meat, and when they succumbed, cut their throats.'

'That's very likely it,' I agreed. 'What's so strange about it?'

He frowned and said: 'You didn't know those dogs. If any stranger had tried to get near them, he'd have felt their teeth, meat or no meat. The inference is that whoever

36

drugged them that night was known and liked by them!'

It merely coincided with what I had already seen. But I still felt that same helpless horror as I had when I had spotted June's wet shoes and recently used raincoat.

Archie said: 'What do you think now?'

'I can't say. I don't dare think. All we can do is keep our eyes open, and if — if by any chance it is a — a person we know and like, do what we can to — to cure her of this horrible obsession.'

'As a doctor,' Archie said, 'what would you say mental afflictions, such as the one which possesses this witch-woman, are caused by? I mean, what would make a woman do such terrible things?'

'Repression mainly,' I told him. 'But there may be other causes. I should say the afflicted person commits the crimes in a state of somnambulism. That's a highbrow word for sleep-walking. As I see it, she would retain indistinct memories of her activities when the spell has passed. To her they would seem almost like the disjointed images of dreams.'

'I see.' He broke off for a moment as he

remembered something. 'If a woman had shut herself away from the society of young men of her own age for years, dreaming and waiting for one man to return to her, would you call that repression?'

'I would definitely,' I told him. 'What's this leading up to?'

Archie shifted his feet uncomfortably. 'Well, until these horrible things started happening, June couldn't think or talk of anyone except you. She was just living for the day when you'd come back to her. But she kept it to herself. I was the only one who knew how desperately she needed someone who was unattainable.'

'And you think that because of that she might be the witch-woman,' I said, horrified, even though he was only confirming my own terrible suspicions.

* * *

Derek Denham arrived late with Colonel Merton. His train had been delayed for hours, and it was not until just before dinner that I saw him. There was little time then for conversation, but I liked him immediately.

He was a tall, strapping red-headed young man of great culture and charm. There was about him the tang of the wide open spaces. If he had been dressed in chaps and a Stetson, he would have made an excellent hero for any rough-riding cowboy movie. He was devoted to April, that was evident. His eyes scarcely left her from the moment she met him until we trooped in for dinner.

It was a gloomy meal. An air of foreboding seemed to hang over everyone, even the servants. Derek Denham had heard the tale of the witch by now, and even he seemed visibly affected. Archie, poor fellow, did try to liven the meal up, but failed miserably. Only April was calm and untroubled, laughing and joking and sparkling with gaiety. June was silent and pale-faced, and immediately after dinner excused herself and went back to her room again.

We all turned in early. I think we were becoming bored with ourselves and each other, and were only too glad of the chance of being alone with our own thoughts.

It must have been an hour after the household had retired to bed, and exactly eleven-fifteen by my watch, when I decided to slip along and see if June was still awake. After what Archie had told me that day, I felt sure I could discover the reason for her stubborn coldness towards me. At the risk of a nasty snub, I tapped gently upon her door. There was no reply, but the light, as on the previous night, was still burning. I knocked louder. Then I tried the door handle. It was locked.

I blush to confess my next action. Carried away by my fear of what might be happening to June, I stooped and put my eye to the keyhole. The room, so far as I could see, was entirely empty.

Something like panic gripped me. Obviously June had left her room. For what? Was she still in the house? I doubted that, because, if so, why should she lock her door? Why should she leave the light burning as if she were in the room? And if she were outside, what was she doing? My mind and heart revolted from the theory which circumstances presented. But even if she were not the witch-woman, was she not in terrible danger?

With that thought, action came. I hurried back to my room, donned my clothes and shoes, and heedless of coat or hat, moved rapidly out into the night.

The moon was smiling down on the peaceful countryside, and from the stables nearby came the hooting of a solitary owl. Away down the drive, the rutted track leading on to the moor could be seen.

Treading along it swiftly was the figure of a woman in a light raincoat.

I started after her, discarding the idea of calling June's name. If she were sleep-walking, it might be harmful to awaken her suddenly.

When I had reached the summit of the hill and could look down into the depth of the sloping moors, I was amazed at the distance she had put between us. I began to run, heading towards the part of the moor where those small, stunted trees told of the presence of the dreaded Pikeville bog.

Before I had covered half the distance, she vanished into the trees. I ran on, panting slightly, perspiration dewing my forehead. As I drew nearer the trees, I noticed a woman walking carefully along, skirting the edge of the bog. I put on speed and called: 'June, June!' At all costs I must stop her sleep-walking into the bog.

The figure paused, and I saw it was not, after all, June. Although the coat the woman wore was similar in appearance, she was plump and chubby, with fat, red cheeks and tousled hair. I came up to her, gasping.

'Have you seen anyone — anyone about here?' I asked. She was ill at ease, but at the sound of my voice she smiled and said:

'Phew! Bless me if I didn't think you were one of them men I hear about who go round attacking ladies!'

'You can rest assured on that point. I'm quite respectable.'

'Well I ain't seen nobody, mister, not since I left my young man, I 'aven't.' She gave me a coquettish smile and a veiled glance from her eyes. It struck me that had I been one of the men she had mentioned, she would not have been exactly averse to my advances.

'Aren't you out here rather late?'

'Ay, I am, mister. My father, Ben Salter — I'm Sally Salter —'e'd leather me if 'e knew. I'm counting on sneaking in without 'im hearing me. I meanter say, a woman's got to 'ave a bit of fun, ain't she?'

'What brings you out here at this time of the night, Miss Salter?' I asked suspiciously.

'I've been telling you — me young man, 'im as lives over at Marshton. Father don't approve of him, and we have to meet on the q.t. I've been over there, and we went to the pictures. That made us late. Then we had an argument, and he left me to walk home all on my owney-oh.'

I didn't think much of her young man for that, whoever he was. But I wasn't there to dwell on the merits or demerits of the local swains. I went on: 'Aren't you afraid of these rumours about a witch-woman?'

'Lor' bless you, mister, no. I'll be home in next to no time, and I'm a rare runner if I should see 'er. Besides, I bet I could give 'er as good as I got. I'm ever so strong, feel!'

I coughed. 'Just the same I'd better walk a little way with you.'

'That's O.K. by me, mister,' she replied, and again her eyes hinted that she wouldn't be averse to sitting down in the shadows for a while during that walk. But at that moment I thought I detected a shadow in the woods behind her, and I said: 'On second thoughts, if you hurry, you should be quite safe.'

Before she could retort, I had broken past her into the trees at the densest point. I was sure I had seen someone move there.

The wood grew thicker and I became hopelessly lost. Then suddenly I burst from the trees and stumbled into the open. I stood there trying to get my bearings, and realised that I was facing the road which ran into the village.

Then, from the right, behind a clump of trees, came a shrill, blood-chilling shriek! It ended on a suffocating, gurgling note, as if the one who uttered it were screaming through a throat congested with blood. When the scream died, the silence was horrible. Picking my way with care, I rounded the trees, and reeled back in horror at the dreadful thing I saw.

5

Murder Most Horrible

It was enough to make anyone stagger — even men with far steadier nerves than mine.

There, clearly illuminated by the vivid moonlight, lay the woman with whom I had so recently talked — Sally Salter. Her throat was a ghastly, red gash; her eyes were glazed with the gloss of death; her face was contracted in horror, every feature screwed up, and seeming only half the size of a normal face.

Near the mutilated body was a young woman, sobbing. I could have wept myself when I saw that the sobs came from June. She knelt down beside the body, tears rolling down her cheeks.

June's grief was horrible to see, and I guessed it was another symptom of her dangerous mental digressions. I was now convinced that the witch-woman knelt before me, although the weapon with which she had committed her appalling crime wasn't in sight.

I was wary. The chances were that when she knew of my presence, June would turn on me and treat me in the same way as she had treated that dreadful body which lay under the pale Somerset moon.

June glanced up, and her wild eyes met mine. She showed no fury. She simply stared at me, numbed with a hopeless horror.

I said: 'June! What made you do it?'

'Me? Alan! You don't think — you can't think that I —' She rose to her feet, wiping away her tears, and took a step towards me. I in turn took a step back.

'What else can I think? I find you here like this —'

'But would I be here if I'd done this? Wouldn't I have run off?'

'Possibly your attack had worn off. Perhaps you suddenly came to a realisation of what you had done. June, I only want to help you. A long rest in a nursing home, and you would soon —'

'You fool ...' Her voice seemed to be on the verge of bursting with strain. 'How could you ever have suspected me? Hadn't it ever struck you that I might be trying to help someone myself? Didn't you think of that?'

'I don't understand ... Help someone? Who?'

'I came out here ... Oh, I can't explain yet. Listen, Alan. We can't help this poor woman. She's dead now. I'm going to ask you to do me one big favour — bigger than ever you've done for me in the past. If you truly love me, you'll do it. I can't offer you any reward, and I can't promise that it will make any difference between us. But I want you to believe that I didn't kill Sally Salter — that I am as innocent as you are. I want you to promise to keep this to yourself. Please, Alan. Let someone else find the body. We'll tell the police nothing. In return, I'll promise to see that no more of these — these atrocities take place. Promise me, Alan.'

'Good heavens! Do you realise what you're asking, June?'

'You don't trust me. You still believe I did this.'

I grunted. 'Did you see who did do it?'

'No, but I suspect someone. That's why I want you to forget all this. Forget you ever saw me here. If you tell, I can't prevent suspicion falling on myself, and though I might be kept under lock and key, the guilty person would still be at large. Don't you see? The fiend would be free to attack other people! Look, Alan, I promise if this should happen again to tell you everything I suspect.'

The tears streamed down her cheeks again. The sight of her touched me deeply. She begged, pleaded and cajoled. When she saw I was weakening, she came near and put her hands on my arms. Heaven help me; I knew I was in her power. There was something magnetic about her.

I tried to bluster. 'I'll keep my mouth shut,' I said, 'only on the condition that you help us to catch the witch-woman red-handed.'

She nodded, tears still glistening on her cheeks. Try as I might, I could not believe that June would kill another woman. On the other hand, if I had done my duty and told the police what I had seen, she might have told what she knew, and so prevented other people being horribly murdered.

But love was blinding me to common sense. Like two conspirators, we covered the woman's poor face with her raincoat and went back to the lodge. All the way, I tried to persuade June to tell me what she knew and whom she suspected. But she steadfastly shook her head, saying she was not yet sure and might be doing someone a grave injustice. I couldn't see this, but I took her word for it like a blind fool, and when we said good night at her bedroom door, I was still no nearer a solution of the mystery.

The next morning saw the arrival of a stout and foreboding visitor to the lodge. Police-constable William Ezra Jerms, red-faced and officious, called on us to ask a few questions. He asked them while he sucked his right thumb and made illiterate marks with a stub of pencil in his notebook.

'None o' you 'eard nor saw anything?' he demanded, and I felt like a guilty man as I dissented with the others.

April said: 'For heaven's sake, Jerms, how on earth could we possibly hear anything from here? The murder happened almost a mile away.'

'That be so, miss, but I got me dooty to do, an' I means to do h'it, with your permission.'

'Carry on, Jerms,' Colonel Merton said. 'Your question was quite a sensible one.'

'Thank ye, sir. I won't detain you long. Like as not, the chief of police from Bath'll be wanting to ask ye questions when 'e h'arrives. They might even call in Scotland Yard,' he went on impressively. 'It ain't often we gets a real juicy murder down here.'

'You think it was a straightforward murder? Not the work of the witch-woman?' enquired June slowly.

'Depends how you looks at it, miss,' Jerms said portentously. 'But I can tell you what I think. I think it was supernatural work, I do. But I'll not be telling the chief I think that. Like as not, 'e'd say I wasn't fit to have charge of Pikeville if 'e knew I believed in spooks.'

The P.C., who had evidently seen fairies at the bottom of his garden, left after asking a few minor questions. Indeed, it was clear his visit had not been inspired as much by the hope of learning any fresh facts, as by his desire to appear important in the eyes of Dalia, the cook, with whom — Mary told us — he had what the Sunday newspapers politely call an illicit alliance.

At two-forty that afternoon, a stout and frightened-looking woman whizzed through the door, accompanied by the second maid, and headed briskly in the direction of Pikeville. Dalia, the cook, was leaving; and although Mary, the first maid, had avowed her intention of staying on, she still followed the cook's retreat with somewhat wistful eyes.

It was indeed a terrible roof to live under, and with the additional knowledge I possessed I found it almost intolerable. If we had received a visit from any intelligent members of the police force, I would have been induced, I'm sure, to tell my secret to them, even at the risk of estranging myself from June.

There was an unexpected diversion later that day. While we sat on the lawn in deck chairs, each busy with his own thoughts, Calantini suddenly turned in from the road, looking more than ever like an out-of-work repertory actor.

He swept across the lawn towards us, announcing himself with the words: 'I am here — Calantini in person.'

The expression on Derek's features — who had not so far met the great man — was ludicrous. He glanced at us quizzically and scratched his red hair.

April muttered: 'Curse the man!'

Calantini fixed his eyes immediately upon Derek, and striding over until he towered above the deck chair, barked: 'No doubt you are this Derek Denham.'

'No doubt I am,' agreed Derek. 'I haven't the pleasure of knowing you, have I?'

'It will be no pleasure, I assure you,' grunted Calantini.

Archie hastily put himself between them, and introduced with mock formality: 'Mr. Calantini — Mr. Denham, April's *fiancé.*'

'*Pah!*' snorted Calantini, and his soft voice packed a great deal of venom into the exclamation. 'Now I wonder more than ever why it is she preferred such as you to such as me.'

'I beg your pardon?' said Derek, a dangerous undertone in his voice.

'I say, I now wonder even more why she

did not choose Calantini. But no! I do not wonder. I know ... It is because she is a fool, just as you are a fool! All fools!'

'Very interesting,' growled Derek, rising to his feet and clenching his ham-like hands.

'I repeat: Calantini is not afraid of such as you. I say you are a fool. She is fool —'

'You're rather a fool yourself,' observed Archie. 'You're fool enough to be putting yourself in line for a nasty smack on the nose. Shall I, or will you, Derek?'

Derek waved Archie aside and said: 'My prerogative, I think.'

'You will not dare to touch Calantini,' the Italian blustered. 'Calantini will kill!' As if by sleight of hand, he flashed a long knife.

Derek gave a perceptible frown. His foot shot up, and the knife spun into the air and came to rest yards away. Derek advanced grimly. 'You're making yourself obnoxious,' he commented. 'Scram or you'll get it.'

'You would not dare! You think she loves you. *Pah!* She loves *any* man, that one. She is a —' He spat out a word which neither I nor Derek could understand. But the sound of it was enough, and Calantini got just what he'd been asking for.

Derek's fist drew back, and Calantini's protest was cut off abruptly as he received a knobbly set of knuckles planted upon the end of his prominent nose. He roared with pain and rose three inches from the lawn. Derek then grasped him swiftly and purposefully by the rear of his tight trousers and propelled him violently towards the gate.

'Release me! Let me go, I say! How dare you do this to Calantini?'

A hefty boot landed enthusiastically upon his trousers at the tightest point, and Calantini flew into the road like a startled chicken, rolling over in the dust.

'Goal!' yelled Archie. 'Well played, Derek old top.'

Calantini picked himself up and glared over the gate. He shook an enraged fist and shouted: 'For this you will pay! Calantini will kill you!' Then, his ears ringing with Archie's laughter, he strutted off down the road. Derek turned back to his chair and sank into it as if nothing had happened.

But April was uneasy. 'You don't believe what Calantini said, do you Derek? There was no truth in it. He never had any promise of marriage from me.'

'Of course I don't believe it, darling,' said Derek with a smile. 'The man is just cracked. Anyone can see that. Forget it.'

But I was a little disturbed. I said: 'He looks as crazy as a coot, but personally I'd give him credit for having more brains than one would think. Don't forget, he's written some very clever books on psychology.'

'He's just plain barmy,' laughed Archie. 'Would any sane man act the way he does?'

'Many sane men would if they had the fiery Latin temperament,' I said. 'Not all races are as undemonstrative as Englishmen. If I were you, Derek, I'd be on my guard for Calantini. Did you notice how he drew that knife — as if it were second nature for him to use it? I wouldn't disregard his threats too much. He may look like the villain from an old-fashioned melodrama, but believe me, there's plenty of danger in his eyes.'

Derek nodded and said he'd look out for vipers in his bed. I could see he refused to take my warning seriously. But I wasn't the only person who was perturbed. June was also.

She drew me aside when the others started a game of croquet and said: 'Alan, do you really think Calantini might — might try to carry out his threat?'

'I do. There's something sinister about the man, for all his silly boastfulness and queer dress — something that makes me think he'd be a dangerous enemy.'

'I've noticed it, too. It's in his eyes, isn't it? They're — they're — oh, I can't describe them!'

We were interrupted by Archie, who came bustling over and suggested tennis before tea. We agreed readily. Anything would be better than sitting around and brooding. June went to change and rejoined us on the court. Derek sat it out, laughingly, saying that Calantini had given him enough sport for one day.

As we left the court, I drew June aside again and skilfully whisked her away from the others. She made no protest, but allowed me to guide her to the old tree on which, so long ago, we had carved our names inside an arrow-pierced heart. We stood looking at them, unchanged, timeless, enduring. We were both carried back over the years, it seemed, back to that last night together before I had gone abroad. With a sudden sob, June was nestling tightly in my arms again, as she had then, and my lips were pressing down to hers.

I held her very tightly, and loved her with all my soul. Yes, I would have given my soul for her — even if she were the witch-woman.

6

June — The Truth!

She was mine again. She gave herself to me with complete spiritual surrender. Her soft, yielding body braced hard against me. Her warm red lips clung to mine as if they would never leave me. It was as I had wanted her all those seven years. The years of separation seemed to vanish, as if they had never been. There was only June, myself and the garden, and the wonder of our love waiting to be fulfilled.

I found myself holding her with an almost brutal intensity that I could not lessen.

'June darling, we must be married. We can't risk any more misunderstandings.'

Yes, I asked that of the lovely creature whom some people suspected of being the witch-woman. A wild, surging passion had seized me, dulling all reason. I was jubilant that at last the barrier which those seven years seemed to create had been removed.

'Please, Alan — don't make love to me, and please, please don't ask me to marry you.'

For a moment I could neither move nor speak, so intense was my disappointment. Then I grasped her firmly by the shoulders and tilted her tear-stained face to mine.

'June, snap out of it. You love me, don't you?' She nodded silently. 'Then what on earth is there to stop us getting married?'

'Something personal. I can't tell you. Honestly, Alan, you mustn't ask.'

'But I have a right to know! Heavens, do you mean to say you'd turn me down without telling me what stands between us?'

She thought for a long time. At least it seemed a long time to me while I waited for her reply with a sinking sensation in the pit of my stomach. Finally she whispered: 'Yes, Alan, I suppose you have the right to know. I can trust you. So I'll tell you ... I can't marry you because I suspect there's insanity in my family. Oh, wasn't it plain why I was so cold to you? I didn't want this to happen. I didn't want you to start loving me as I loved you. I knew that if we began, then the parting, when it came, must be harder. I knew that you would be hurt, and I would find it more difficult to do the right thing. So, you see, I just wanted us to drift apart.'

'June darling, I don't care if your entire family are raving lunatics. You know that. I'd marry you if the colonel thought he was Napoleon himself.'

'It isn't as amusing as that.' All the colour had drained from her face. 'I told you I suspect someone of being the witch-woman. The someone I suspect is — April!'

I took this calmly. I had expected it. Not that I found it easily believable; but if the witch-woman were not June, there seemed no alternative. April was the only other woman who fitted the witch-woman's description. I said quietly: 'Tell me about it, dear.'

She began to speak hurriedly, as if she were almost ashamed of saying what she did against her own sister. 'My suspicions started soon after the first reports of the witch-woman came in,' she told me. 'One night, a week later, I happened to go to April's room for a book. She wasn't there. Her heavy shoes were missing too, and the pillows were arranged in the bed to look like a sleeping person. I was worried, but not unduly so. You see, I knew she'd been meeting a number of the young men from surrounding houses late at night while Derek was away. I don't suppose there's any harm in it, but naturally she didn't want it to come to the ears of her fiancé. That's why I've been so secretive about the whole thing. If it were harmless affairs she goes out for, I'd feel terrible if I exposed her.

'That first night you came, I followed her, trying to find out where she really went. If I had discovered she really was the witch-woman, I'd have put the matter in Father's hands. But I never did find out for sure. I lost her, just as I lost her last night, when you followed me. That's why I didn't want you to say anything, Alan, because I should either have had to tell what I knew, or take the blame myself. If I'd told and it had turned out April was quietly conducting a silly intrigue with one of the farmer's sons, I'd have felt awful: I'd have ruined her entire life, because she really does worship Derek, whatever she may do to pass the time until she marries him.'

She pressed a tight hand to her forehead. 'I'm beginning to think I was wrong in getting you to keep it to yourself. I'm beginning to think I should have told what I knew when I first suspected. I'm almost sure it's April now; that's why I can't marry you, Alan. It wouldn't be fair to — to any children we might have.'

'June, you *must* marry me! We aren't sure it *is* April. At least let's wait until we know — and even if it is, we can still marry. Probably April's condition was aggravated by repression.'

'April? Repressed? Far from it! She's always done exactly as she wished, except that Father wouldn't let her live in London.'

I was ready to seize at a straw.

'That's it. Don't you see? If a person's mind is at all unstable, a small thing like that would do the trick. The mind's an odd thing, June. Being forced to live down here, in the heart of a quiet stretch of country, would do strange things to any woman who longed for the bright lights and wanted to be the life and soul of every party.'

'Yes, Alan, but not unless her brain was already slightly unbalanced. You must admit that.'

I had to. Repressions can cause queer warps, but they cannot cause a normal person to drink human blood.

The more I argued with June, the more stubborn she became. She would not marry me if the witch-woman proved to be April. That was final. Personally I was not at all sure it could be April. The fact that she had been out when the crimes had been committed was circumstantial evidence — evidence upon which the police could not convict unless there were something to corroborate it. I said as much to June, and asked her when April usually went out. Was it every night?

'Most nights,' said June. 'Certainly every time I've kept watch for her, she's gone. Oh, Alan, we'd better tell what we know. It isn't fair to keep it to ourselves now. Let's telephone the police before she does any more harm.'

'No,' I said suddenly. 'Not yet. I've got a better idea ... Which way does she leave the house?'

'Always by the rear entrance — through the kitchen.'

'Then here's what we'll do. Tonight I'll wait in the kitchen. If April comes through, I'll follow her. It'll be embarrassing for me if she is only meeting some local Romeo, but I can always sneak away, and then her secret won't leak out and spoil her marriage. On the other hand, if she betrays any signs of a woman who's hell-bent on murder, I'll stop her before she has a chance to kill.'

'Alan! You can't do that. If she is — is insane, she might kill you!'

'Don't you believe it,' I said grimly. 'I'm not Sally Salter, and it'll be *she* who's taken by surprise, not me. No, darling, I'll be safe enough. But I hope to heaven it's just an intrigue, and not anything to worry unduly about.'

We went inside after arranging other details. After June had powdered her nose, we joined the others at dinner a little late, but nothing was said.

After dinner, Derek, Archie, the colonel and I played snooker in the billiard room. The game broke up soon afterwards, and Derek wandered off to find April. June was in the library, looking moodily through a heavy volume titled 'Diseases of the Brain.' I steered her out into the garden, took her hand and pressed it gently.

'Don't worry, June. I feel sure everything will be plain sailing. Ten to one, if April should leave the house tonight, it'll be just to keep a rendezvous with someone. Anyway, we'll know for certain what's what and who's who.'

'I hope so. It's the uncertainty that makes me feel so awful. If we knew for sure, we could perhaps do something for her. But as it is, we're just playing a horrible kind of blind man's buff.'

Somehow we forced the subject to the back of our minds, and the next ten minutes, although overshadowed, were the happiest I had spent since my arrival at Merton Lodge. When we returned to the lodge, the others were getting ready for bed. We surprised April and Derek in the library as they engaged in a passionate embrace. The huddle was revealingly passionate so far as April was concerned. I began to understand what June had meant when she said April had been carrying on intrigues with husky young farmers while Derek was away. She was man-crazy.

When they saw us, they jumped up guiltily and pretended to be searching for some book or other. When we said good night, they said they thought they'd push off to bed, too. Looking at April as she went up the stairs ahead of me — her tiny feet beating a tattoo on the woodwork, her slim legs, and the babyish roundness of the back of her knees, I could not believe that here was a murderess ... April, of the laughing eyes and ready wit, the sleek hair and white, even teeth, the inviting red lips and subtly curved body! Surely she could not have done those shocking deeds that lay like a ghastly spectre so near to the gates of Merton Lodge?

No, it was too fantastic to be true. Nevertheless, as soon as silence had claimed the lodge, I slipped from my room again, down the old stairs and into the kitchen. I took up a position behind the larder door. The place was in a riot of disorder, left that way when Dalia, the cook, had hurriedly deserted her post hours earlier. I rummaged round until I found what I wanted — a neat but heavy rolling pin. I intended to be prepared.

Here, in the silent lodge, with the whole place in deep gloom, anything seemed possible. It did not seem so unbelievable that April could be the witch-woman in the dead of night, with only the mournful hoot of the owl on the stable roof to break the gaunt stillness of the house and the grounds.

But as I stood listening, other sounds gradually became audible: scuffling, gnawing noises, such as mice make; creaking woodwork; and somewhere in the kitchen the monotonous dripping of a leaky tap. My own breathing seemed to fill the room, and the hammering of my heart was like the beating of a tom-tom.

Then, from the direction of the passage which led to the house itself, there came the stealthy slur of a slippered foot!

My grip on the rolling pin tightened. Irrelevantly I thought of trifling things, things that helped to stave off my own fear — things like irate wives crowning inebriated husbands with just such a handy household utensil as I proposed to use for grimmer purposes, if necessary.

The steps paused at the door. I tried to stifle my breathing.

'Alan.'

It was June's voice. My breath burst in a gasp of relief. I murmured softly: 'June, I'm here, behind the larder door.'

She glided forward like a ghost. She was wearing her nightgown, covered by a dressing robe. She sought my hand in the darkness, and only the shimmering outlines of her face and figure were visible in the gloom. I felt the hard, squat shape of a small pistol pressed into my hand, and she murmured: 'Just in case, Alan.'

'Thanks. Anything happening?'

'No. I listened when I passed April's door. She seemed to be fast asleep. There was no light. I heard her breathing deeply. Perhaps she won't go out tonight. If it was an intrigue, she wouldn't dare to carry it on with Derek actually in the house. Or would she?'

'She might, but if it isn't an intrigue, I'd better wait a little longer.'

I had scarcely got the words out of my mouth than a hoarse, echoing scream tore through the house. It was a man's voice.

'Good God!' I gasped. 'What the devil …?'

Then I ran full-tilt into the hall and up the stairs. June wasn't far behind. We tried Archie's room first. He was just struggling into his dressing gown. He, too, had heard.

'The cry seemed to come from Derek's room,' he explained.

In the passage we were joined by Colonel Merton and Mary, the maid.

Derek was lying in bed, dead. His arms were thrown up as if to ward off an enemy who had vanished. His throat was horribly slashed!

7

The Witch-Woman Shows Herself

We clustered in the doorway, too horrified to move. Archie's bull-frog eyes were glazed. The colonel was white. June's head was buried in her desolate hands. I was cursing my stupidity in assuming that April would naturally seek her victims outdoors. She had done before. Why hadn't I foreseen that she might change her ghastly technique?

It was upon this scene that April came. Where she came from, none of us could be certain. One moment there were just the five of us — Mary the maid was sobbing outside the door — and the next moment April was standing there, gazing with blank eyes into the room.

The colonel saw her first and shuddered at the sight of his own daughter. There was something weird about her expression, as if she were dead to all about her; as if, too, her mind had snapped under the strain, and self-possession had suddenly deserted her.

It was a look I had seen before. I tried to remember where, and what it implied.

The colonel, overwrought, obviously, feared for her sanity. He thought she had seen the corpse of her fiancé, and that this was the direct result. He stepped to her side, seized her arm, shook her, and said hoarsely: 'April, my dear, don't give way.'

Like one coming from a deep dream, her eyes moved slightly. She stared at her father, recognition dawning in her eyes. Her lips trembled convulsively as she said: 'Where am I? How did I get here?'

Receiving no immediate answer from her father, her eyes began to quest about the room, passing each of us in turn with a look of bewilderment. Again she spoke. 'What's happened? Why are you all here?'

I realised she had not yet seen the body of her fiancé; I now felt sure she did not retain any impression of having killed him. Then I remembered where I had seen that strange somnambulistic look before — in a hospital at Lin-Yutang, in the eyes of a person who had been hypnotised!

I stepped forward quickly to take her arm and guide her out before she saw that dreadful sight on the bed. But I was too late. Her wandering eyes found the bed and rested on the mutilated body.

I hope that, as long as I live, I may never again hear a scream such as escaped her, or see another expression like the one which twisted her features. In China I have seen some heartbreaking displays of grief, and a doctor becomes more or less hardened to them. But never have I seen a face so warped and contorted with suffering as April's at that moment. Never have I heard a woman's voice ring out in such a high-pitched, unearthly scream. It ripped from her lips and echoed around the room, piercing and unrestrained. While we stood there, too numbed and shocked to move, her legs buckled under her and she crashed helplessly to the floor, completely senseless.

Colonel Merton picked his daughter up in strong arms, carried her to her room, laid her on the bed and tried smelling salts. It was useless. Her breathing was deep and even, but she showed no signs of recovery.

As a doctor, I tried to diagnose while

the colonel waited anxiously, twisting his fingers in despair. 'It's shock,' I said finally. 'A mild form of epilepsy.'

'Epilepsy?' gasped the colonel. 'But she's never suffered from anything like this before.'

I looked at him compassionately. Not for the world would I have broken it to him at that moment that the witch-woman was his daughter. It would have killed him.

'There's nothing to worry about,' I said as cheerfully as I could. 'Let her rest. She'll soon come round. Does her own doctor live far away?'

'About five miles,' he said dully.

'Then I advise you to send for him. He knows her better than I. No doubt he'll be able to prescribe for her.'

'She'll get better, won't she, Doctor?' he begged, using my professional title in his agitation.

'Perfectly. You need have no immediate fears for her. She'll sleep now for quite a long time.'

'Then I'll go and get the doctor in my car,' he said. 'I'll phone him now and tell him to be ready to come along. He's rather old, and he won't be able to manage the drive himself at night.'

'What about calling the police?'

'Oh, yes. But Jerms' phone is out of order. Perhaps Archie would go.'

Within a few minutes the big, gaunt house was empty except for Mary, the maid, June and myself. June stared at me uncertainly and we sent Mary, trembling, back to bed.

Then I motioned June out of April's room, turned the key in the lock, and handed it to June. I said: 'Stay here. I don't believe she'll waken yet, but if she does try to get out, you mustn't let her. Your father will be back with the doctor in no time. I have somewhere I must go.'

'*Go?* Alan, you can't *leave* me. Not here alone.'

'I must, darling. Calantini may clear out. He must know he's gone too far this time.'

'Calantini? I don't understand.'

'Morally, he's a murderer several times over. I was a fool not to have realised it before. When I saw the look in April's eyes tonight, I knew she was hypnotised. Some other stronger will had possession of her, subjugating her own to the extent of entire

been unopened for some time, and it took all my strength to make the needed space. But gradually I slid the stone aside, lowered myself into the darkness, and felt for the iron rungs with my feet.

The secret passage had been made during the days of the Cromwell regime, when cavaliers had used my old home for a meeting place. Old records in the town told of many daring escapes through that tunnel; but never, I think, could any cavalier have pushed down the tunnel as eagerly as I did.

Now all would be plain sailing if only the secret spring at the other end, leading into the library, still worked. I fumbled along until I reached the steep stone steps. I went up them, carefully now, for I could not yet be sure if Calantini was in the library.

When I reached the stout oak panel, I moved aside a small piece of wood which covered a knothole. This had been used long years ago as a spyhole. The shades of those long-dead cavaliers seemed to be with me as I peered into the deserted library. Ghostly voices seemed to echo in my ears, whispering encouragement.

I pressed the button which worked the panel, and it slid noiselessly aside. I stepped through into the library of my old home. The furnishing, as June had said, was unchanged. Exactly the same articles were precisely in the same position.

But now the desktop contained grisly objects: skulls, a crystal globe, and a conical-shaped cap. In a large glass case my torch picked out the stuffed and mummified legs of lizards and frogs. There were several jars of liquids, one containing something which looked like blood plasma. In fact, all the paraphernalia of a man who dabbled in higher witchcraft were now in this room where I had spent many childhood hours. It was a sorcerer's den!

But my interest didn't lie in these things. I made at once for the desk. Here there was a secret drawer, its operation revealed in the deeds of the house. To one who knew nothing of its whereabouts, it would never even have been suspected. But I knew its exact position, and just how to open it. That was something Calantini would not have bargained for.

The drawer opened to my touch, and

from it I drew a long scroll of parchment. I spread it over the desk and shone my torch on it. My breath almost whistled from my lips; it was more damning evidence of Calantini's evil intentions than I had ever reckoned on securing.

Unable to to resist, I began to read. It was penned in a fine, sloping hand, and was wholly written in Latin. I had reason to bless my training as a medical student, for I was now able to read that strange document with ease.

'I, Calantini, have conceived an experiment which should prove of great interest. I will publish the facts in my next book if my power proves as strong as I believe.

'There must be a subject, and I have selected a woman — a woman who has spurned me. For this reason, I have chosen that she will be the one to unwittingly assist in my researches.

'How strong is the power of hypnotism? How far will the mind of a great hypnotist reach out to make its subject do its will? These are things I plan to answer, for never before have I put my powers to such a use.

'Can the subject of a hypnotic trance,

once in my spell, be ruled at my will ever after that, without further contact with me? I shall see ...'

Here the writing broke off, and the next entry was in slightly darker ink, as though it had been written later.

'It is indeed so. Last night I contrived to be alone with April Merton. She was not a hard subject to control. Once I had her in my power, once her will gave place to mine, I withdrew, ordered her to make her memory blank, go to the edge of the lake and unloose the mooring rope of the punt there. I watched her from cover and saw that she obeyed my instructions implicitly.

'I returned home, and at a little after one o'clock in the morning I ordered her to leave the house stealthily, first putting on her shoes. I brought her to me at this place, and here I gave her a knife which was long and sharp. Then I sent her out to kill. For the first step in my experiment, her order was to kill a sheep. She carried this out perfectly, later hiding the weapon, cleaning her shoes, and returning to bed. When she wakes, her memory will be a blank ... Such is Calantini's revenge!

(Later) 'It is now two weeks since April Merton came under my control. The simple dolts hereabouts now believe there is a witch at large — and they are right.

'I have used her as I pleased: the dogs at her home have fallen to her knife, as well as hens and sheep. Soon will come the next step — a human life.'

Here followed a blank page, and then the madman's narrative was renewed:

'She has killed her first human victim; a peasant woman. So my will can make her go to the extreme ... My power is limitless. Tonight will come the final stage. Can my will triumph over her love? We shall soon see. I plan to use my telepathic powers to make her murder her own fiancé. When this is done, my experiment and my vengeance will have run their courses, except for one last stage — *her own suicide*!'

It was a hideous plan, bred in a brain warped with hate and sadistic desire. I began to roll up the document. Then I jumped in panic as the light was switched on. Calantini was standing in the doorway, gripping a business-like automatic.

8

Death Rattle

'This is an unusual time to pay Calantini a social call,' he said with suave menace. 'But Calantini is hospitable, yes? Sit down, my friend, and tell me what you do with Calantini's important document?'

I sat down abruptly. In the face of that gun there was little else I could do. I chose the swivel chair behind the desk, and Calantini walked forward until he stood about three feet away from me.

The gun in his hand looked business-like, and although I did not by any means count this as the end of the game, I awaited my chance patiently. He seemed in a talkative mood. His mad genius was thirsty for praise and admiration. He wanted me to admit he was clever. He said blandly: 'You have read the document? You can understand Latin?'

'I'm a doctor,' I told him. 'So I have read it, and understood it.'

'Is it not very interesting?'

'I found it so. As the outpourings of a madman, it's unique.'

He smiled at this. 'I had feared you would think that. Alas, the world neglects its genius. The world does not understand such men as Calantini. That is why I was forced to leave Italy, where superstition runs even higher than in Britain.

'Public opinion chased me out of my own country, Doctor. What dolts these stupid peasants are! A man of science must always push forward, caring little whom he crushes so long as he attains his object.'

'You call yourself *a man of science?*' I sneered. 'But what particular scientific category does this experiment fall into?'

The automatic trembled in Calantini's hand. 'You are as big a fool as the rest, Doctor. None of you understand. *None!* But *I* know what I am doing. Calantini knows the object he will achieve.'

'The object you will achieve will be the gallows,' I told him. 'Do you imagine, for one instant, that you can get away with this? You fool! Even now your plot is known.' I was about to tell him that June knew, but stopped myself quickly. If he should kill me, what might he do to June? He would kill her to prevent her talking. 'It's known that April is responsible for the murders,' I amended, 'and it won't be long before enquiries are made about me. They must inevitably lead to you, Calantini, since it's also known where I've gone. April is senseless, prostrated by shock, locked in her room, the door guarded. Your schemes are ended.'

He laughed suddenly. 'Why do I worry? They may suspect. But you will be dead before they follow you, and Calantini will be gone, taking with him the parchment you have read. There will be nothing to substantiate the theory that the woman was hypnotised. They will find the knife and the blood-smeared gown she used. My powerful will compelled her to hide them under her wardrobe, by the way. She will be confined to an asylum. I am not yet sure whether it would not be better to make her take her own life,' he said reflectively and cold-bloodedly. 'However, I can decide that in due course. But now I would like the papers you are holding, please.' He leaned forward to take them from my hand.

I started to pass the papers to him. As his hand closed upon them, my fist bunched, swept upward and connected with his jaw. Simultaneously I swiveled the chair to one side. The bullet he fired missed only by an inch. Then he was on me again, and we trampled savagely round the room, fighting like two wildcats. His fingernails raked my face. The glass case crashed to the floor and we fell on top of it among the splinters. The gun flew from his hand, and I scrambled over the floor to reach it. He came after me with a jagged shard of glass from the broken case. I felt the glass rake across my face viciously. Frantically I drove my knee into his groin. He groaned and collapsed.

When he ceased to wriggle, I was standing over him with the gun levelled. 'Get up, Calantini.'

He rose unsteadily. 'What do you propose to do now, Doctor?'

'I shall leave you here, bound, and within the hour you may expect the police.'

I thought I saw a glint of satisfaction in his eyes. He said with suspicious meekness: 'Very well. I can do nothing about that.'

His eyes bored into me. They seemed to

penetrate my brain. A slight mist began to form in front of me. His figure wavered. My mind seemed to be tearing from its moorings. With every effort of willpower, I pulled myself back from the verge of his control. The mist cleared, and he was still there, eyeing me evilly.

'Your hypnotism won't work, Calantini — not on me. I know what you're up to, and I have a will of iron.'

I looked around for some rope to tie him with. His eyes were now fixed and glassy, staring into and beyond the walls of the room. I suspected some fresh devilry, and on an impulse, I determined not to leave him there.

How was I to know he had no servants? How was I to know April was the only one in his spell? If there were another, could he not bring him or her here by his will, and so escape with his victim's aid? I couldn't take any chances.

He was still staring vacantly into space when I cracked the revolver butt neatly over his skull. He went down without a sound.

I stuffed the parchment in my pocket and picked Calantini up. He was quite light, and

I had no difficulty in slinging him over my right shoulder. Then I entered the secret passage again, bending low with my burden.

He showed no signs of regaining consciousness. I was alert for the slightest movement, but none came. He remained dangling limply across my back, his hands thudding against my spine with each step.

Thus I carried the great Calantini to justice — a far swifter and more dreadful justice than I then thought, but one that was far too good for such a sadistic fiend.

As I came near to the end of the pathway through the woods, he suddenly regained his senses, so suddenly that it was clear he had been conscious some minutes, but had been lying low, awaiting his opportunity. Now it had come.

I knew nothing until I felt his fist smack me hard at the nape of the neck. It was a cruel blow, and I stumbled to my knees, half-paralysed. While I lay there in a daze, he kicked me savagely. Then he began to run. He had scarcely covered two yards when the path ended abruptly, and for a mere second he paused, undecided which way to take.

That second's hesitation was disastrous for him. Without warning, from the shadows of the trees a white figure glided behind him. A slender alabaster arm clamped across his face, pulling back his head and stretching his neck taut. Like the blade of a guillotine, a long, keen knife swept down, severing his throat. Then, as if it had never existed, the figure vanished.

I raced to the spot and gulped at the horror I saw. Calantini still lived, but if his life were to be saved, I must immediately get him to the house where I could see the full extent of his injury. I picked him up again, swung him across my shoulder, and started at a run for the rear door.

As I burst onto the lawn, an appalling sight met my eyes. Halfway up the house, clambering to her window by means of the old ivy, was April. Leaning down, gazing with horrified eyes at the knife held between her sister's teeth, was June!

I stood transfixed, staring. Then from behind me I heard a sudden harsh rattling sound that I knew only too well.

Calantini was dead.

The rattle had scarcely left his throat

when the figure on the ivy stopped its climb. Its head turned, and I saw the stark terror in April's face. Then with a wild, throbbing shriek, she lost her grip and crashed onto the hard gravel path thirty feet below.

When I reached her side, nothing could be done; her neck was broken.

The witch-woman was dead. Pikeville was free again from the menace of blood lust.

9

Passionate Rapture

It was seven months later that June and I were married. During the evening before the wedding day, Archie said: 'The mystery of how and why April killed Calantini was never properly cleared up. Have you hit on a solution, Alan?'

'I see it this way,' I said. 'When I got the upper hand of Calantini at his home that night, I told him I meant to tie him up and leave him until I had brought the police. Strangely enough, this seemed to suit him, and I noticed he was doing a lot of staring into space. The devil was concentrating on something. I didn't like it. I didn't guess the truth until later. I thought that possibly he was getting another of his victims to come along and release him. But now I see what he was really doing.

'He had remembered the ivy on the wall at the lodge, and he was willing April to climb down it, lie in wait for me to return, and then kill me. He was clever — *very* clever. He combined hypnotism with telepathy perfectly. It was that unholy combination that made the whole business possible: *normal* hypnotism wouldn't be powerful enough to make anyone act against their own basic nature and kill. But it was a little *too* perfect! As it happened, April followed his instruction to the letter, lying in wait for me at the end of the path through the woods.

'Calantini knew she would. But he hadn't expected me to change my mind and take him with me. Nor did he have a chance to cancel her orders, because I'd knocked him out before he even knew that I'd changed my plans.

'After that, he must have been unconscious most of the time. But as we neared the lodge, he regained his senses, lay low for a few moments, and then knocked me to the ground.

'He began to run. April was waiting. He'd telepathically given her to understand I would be returning that way. You see, he knew my method of entry through the secret passage, and rightly guessed I would go back the same way. What he didn't know was that April, hypnotised as she was, wouldn't be able to see in the darkness exactly *who* she was attacking. She just saw a man, and she probably remembered she'd been instructed to murder a man who came along that path. She did so — before Calantini knew what was happening.'

'The biter bit, eh?' said Archie.

'Exactly!' I agreed. 'It's lucky it happened that way, or there might not have been any wedding tomorrow.'

Archie frowned thoughtfully. 'Poor April suddenly fell like a dead weight from the ivy, didn't she? How do you account for that?'

'When Calantini died, April was no longer under his control. She regained her senses at once. The shock of what was happening sent her hurtling down. It was her second murder that night, remember.'

Archie looked grave for a minute, then he said: 'You know, Alan, I somehow think it was — well, all for the best.'

'I agree with you, Archie. If she'd known what she'd done, her life would have been a misery. At least she was spared the real-isation and remorse.' I drained my glass. 'Well, Archie, I'm off to bed. Tomorrow's the big day.'

★ ★ ★

I found June looking lovelier than ever the following morning. When she saw me in the doorway, she looked horrified.

'Oh, Alan, darling! You shouldn't have come here. It's bad luck to see the bride on the wedding morning.'

'We've had all our bad luck, dear,' I told her. 'From now on it has to be good. Besides, it could never be bad luck to gaze on you at any time.'

She smiled, kissed me and said: 'Flatterer! Very well, I forgive you. But don't do it next time you get married.'

'There won't be any next time,' I assured her.

'You know,' she said, looking at me re-flectively, 'I'm still not sure that I ought to marry you.'

'For mercy's sake, why not? You can't jilt me now.'

'But I'm quite serious. I hate to admit it, but there's still insanity in our family, Alan. Really, there is.'

'Good heavens, June, you aren't serious, are you?'

'But of course I'm serious, Alan, darling. I'm insane myself. I know it. I'm crazy.'

'Crazy to tie yourself to a chump like me?' I said, smiling.

'No, not that, dear. You aren't a chump. You're wonderful. I'm just crazy — about you!'

'In that case we're both crazy,' I said, and my lips came down to meet hers. 'But we won't let that stop us getting married, sweetheart!'

She Vamped a Strangler

1

A Woman's Shame

The ravishing blonde woman crept silently down the wide staircase of the slumbering mansion. Her eyes were wide with fear as, every now and again, a board creaked dismally under her feet. She had to get out before she was seen or heard. It was nearly dawn, and she had been waiting for this chance since midnight.

She clutched her weekend case more firmly and tiptoed on. The front door was locked and chained. It would make too much noise to undo that now. She turned and crept silently down a passage to a baize-covered door at the rear. She didn't know the layout of the place, but she guessed that the door led to the servants' quarters, and she was quite right.

The back door was easier to manipulate. She shot the bolts slowly, opened the door and ran out into the kitchen garden.

Above her the twin towers of the house she was leaving seemed to stare down in the moonlight.

Tears stung her eyes, and she hurried on down the path. She had looked up the trains. There was a milk train leaving at four-thirty. She could be in London, back at her sister's flat, before six. Sandra would wonder about her unexpected return, but Lesley wouldn't be able to face her and tell her the truth. She walked on quickly. No woman would ever have the shame to admit what she had done for diamonds — and the chance of a coronet.

* * *

Miss Green popped her peroxided head of hair round the office door, and directed her horn-rimmed spectacles towards Rodney Granger who was seated at the desk, his feet dumped on the desktop amid a litter of dossiers, old files, broken pens and other odds and ends.

'A young lady,' announced Miss Green, 'to see the eminent private investigator, Rodney Granger.'

Miss Green was being sarcastic. Strictly speaking, Rodney Granger's cases were confined to divorce suits, trailing errant wives at the instructions of equally errant husbands, and keeping an eye on wedding gifts at receptions. His practice, in those respects, was excellent, but he was certainly neither noted nor eminent. He said lazily: 'Young lady? Do I know her?'

'Not yet,' his secretary told him. 'But you'll be glad to when you see her. She's — er — rather pretty. Just the type of client a *wolf* prefers.'

Rodney removed his feet from the desk, straightened one or two pieces of paper, and tidied his desk. 'Then show her in, Miss Green. Hurry!'

Miss Green sniffed sardonically and went back to the outer office. She was replaced by a young woman. Miss Green, in saying she was 'rather pretty', was understating the case. The woman who stood in the doorway, glancing nervously, was utterly beautiful. She had long eyelashes, half-veiling blue eyes, a small retroussé nose, a perfect complexion that made Rodney think of peaches, and a provocatively shaped head of wavy, fair hair.

'Will you step inside, Miss —'

'Lyle — my name is Sandra Lyle. You are Mr. Granger, the private detective?'

'Guilty,' he admitted.

She stepped into the office and closed the door behind her. She sat down gingerly, as if afraid the chair would bite, and thumbed at the clasp of her bag nervously.

Granger noted her apparent anxiety with an expert eye and said: 'Please don't feel alarmed, Miss Lyle. If you have anything of importance to tell me, you can be certain it'll go no further than my own ears.'

She glanced at him quickly. 'How did you know I came to see you about something — something important?'

'Your manner! You seem to be dreadfully worried about something.'

She leaned forward. 'Yes, I'm terribly worried. It's my sister, Mr. Granger. Lesley Lyle. She's — she's gone!'

'Gone?'

'Vanished. She walked out early this morning, and I haven't seen her since.'

'Walked out?'

'Yes. Out of the flat we share.'

Granger looked sympathetic. 'But surely you're worrying unnecessarily, Miss Lyle? If she walked out only this morning, we can hardly assume she's vanished. Least of all that she's come to any harm.'

The woman nodded her fair waves and said: 'I know it must seem like that to you. But it was the circumstances that made me worry. I'll tell you as much as I can about it. Have you ever heard of The Sound of Revelry by Night?'

'Can't say I have. What is it? A new revue?'

'No, Mr. Granger. It's a kind of a night-club and gambling saloon. Lesley — my sister — was the singer there; it was there she met Viscount Sorbo, who's noted for being a bit of a waster and a no-good. But Lesley couldn't see that. She's my kid sister — four years younger than I am. She was flattered and fascinated by the idea of an earl's son being her boyfriend. She went out to parties and to shows with him, and though she certainly didn't love him, she told me he'd be worth marrying for his money. Of course, the idea that he'd ever ask her was quite ridiculous, but she hoped he would.'

'I know how it is,' agreed the detective. 'Please go on.'

'Well, I admit I was surprised myself when she hurried home yesterday afternoon and told me he'd invited her to go down to Marchbrook Towers for the weekend. I could hardly believe it when she packed her best clothes, and without listening to my warnings, left the flat to keep her date with the Viscount, who was driving her down there.

'She got back in the early hours of this morning. She wouldn't tell me anything — not even why she'd come back so soon. She just sat on the edge of the divan, crying her eyes out.

'She cheered up a bit when I suggested going to a show tonight and told her I'd get tickets for the latest play. But when the morning paper arrived, something strange came over her. She got hold of it first and was reading it while I made breakfast. I was in the kitchen for some time, and when I came back she'd gone — packed her own case and mine, too — and left without a word.

'I looked through the paper at once, and

I didn't have to look far. It was clear that the reason for her going was the headline story. Look — I brought the paper along to show you.'

She spread out a paper before him on the desk, and he read:

THEFT AT MARCHBROOK
TOWERS.
BLONDE WOMAN WANTED FOR
QUESTIONING BY THE POLICE.

Last night, Marchbrook Towers, home of the Earl of Marchbrook and his family, was robbed of one of its most priceless heirlooms — a diamond necklace worth fifty thousand pounds. The necklace was presented to the wife of the second Earl of Marchbrook by Queen Elizabeth, for loyal service as a lady-in-waiting, and has remained the family's prize possession for centuries.

The police seem reluctant to say too much about the affair, but we are informed that they wish to trace a blonde woman called Lesley Lyle, once a songstress at The Sound of Revelry by Night, a London nightclub. It is believed this woman was a guest at the Towers at the time of the theft, and has since disappeared. A full description is given below.

Granger laid the paper aside. 'I see! Have the police been to your home?' he asked the crooner's sister.

'Yes, about an hour after Lesley left. Apparently she'd never given Viscount Sorbo her address. Probably she was ashamed of our modest birdcage. The police had quite a time locating me. Well, I simply told them the truth — that she'd gone, and I had no idea where or how.'

'But — but why do you come to me? Surely this is a police job.'

She laid her hand on his arm impulsively and said: 'I want to be quite frank with you, Mr. Granger. In the first place, I came to you because I just can't afford one of the better-known investigators. In the second place, I've heard you are very discreet; and in the third place, I know Lesley wouldn't steal. She's foolish and wayward, but she never did wrong in her life, and I'm sure she never would. I don't know what it's all about, but I want you to trace her for me, and make her come back and face the police!'

Granger looked thoughtful and said: 'But suppose — just suppose — that you're wrong, and that your sister actually is guilty? What then?'

'Then she deserves to face the consequences. But I'm quite certain it isn't like that at all.'

Granger scribbled details on a desk pad, and finally looked up and smiled. 'Very well. If I possibly can, I'll find her for you.'

'Thank you, Mr. Granger. About the fee — I haven't very much.'

He raised his hand in protest. 'We'll discuss that when I've located your sister. It won't be extortionate, Miss Lyle.'

The woman had just gone when Miss Green announced that there was someone else waiting to see Granger. A tall, soldierly -looking man was shown in. To Granger he seemed vaguely familiar. He had the hallmark of British aristocracy and carried himself proudly.

The Earl of Marchbrook smiled and took a seat. He did not appear too eager to broach the subject of his visit, but finally he said: 'Mr. Granger, I know I can rely upon your discretion, sir. I have come to see you on rather a delicate matter, and one which is thoroughly distasteful to me. I must have your full assurance that what I am about to tell you will be in the strictest confidence.'

'You have that, sir.'

'Thank you. I remember you as a very discreet young man. That is why I have chosen to approach you in this matter rather than to go to someone who might be longer established. It concerns my son, the Right Honourable Viscount Sorbo, and since I intend to take you into my confidence, Mr. Granger, let me begin by telling you that my son is neither right nor honourable. It is a hard thing for me, his father, to say, but it is nevertheless perfectly true. My son is a disgrace to the family name. He has no regard for my feelings; he gambles, drinks, consorts with loose women, and gets into every imaginable kind of trouble.

'Recently I cut down his allowance; but he then began to incur extensive bills which were sent to me for payment. I told him that if such a thing should happen again, I would completely disown him, and this threat appeared to have put a stop to his extravagances. Then last night came the unkindest cut. He arrived back from town bringing a nightclub singer to stay for the weekend!'

The old-timer leaned forward. 'Now, I have nothing against nightclub singers, Mr. Granger. Please don't think I'm a snob. But we have a number of eminent people with us at the Towers at the moment, and you will readily admit that a woman of Miss Lesley Lyle's type was hardly in keeping with the company. I must admit that my wife and I were rather cool towards her, and we gave our son to understand that he must send her away the first thing in the morning. But as it happened, that was not necessary. When we rose, not only had the woman gone, but the famous Marchbrook necklace had gone with her!

'I sent for the police, of course, and not wishing it generally known that we numbered nightclub singers amongst our guests, I asked them to keep details out of the papers. To a certain extent they did so, but the midday edition contained a brief account of the theft and stated the police wished to question a blonde woman in connection with the matter.'

Granger nodded. 'I know. I saw that account.'

'Quite so. My son, of course, takes the matter quite calmly. He doesn't seem to think he's to blame in any way for bringing the woman to our home. I really think he wishes the woman good luck in her escape!'

Granger nodded and jotted down a few details on his pad. 'You're quite sure it was the woman who took the necklace?'

'Quite. We have an extensive system of burglar alarms at the Towers. No one could break in from the outside. This morning we found the servant's door open and the woman gone. The glass case, where we keep the necklace in the trophy room, was also opened. Since the house could not be broken into, we never bothered to put the necklace in the safe. The case which contained it was of the flimsiest wood, and had been prised open, apparently with an iron bar.'

'What do you want me to do about it, sir?'

'I want you to find that wretched woman for me, Mr. Granger. I don't want the police to find her first. If they did, they would prosecute, and unpleasant details of how my son invited her down to the Towers would leak out. You understand?'

'I think I do. If you can recover the stolen property, you won't prosecute?'

'Exactly. I would prefer to keep the whole affair out of the newspapers. My son has already figured in far too many disreputable cases.'

Granger stood up and said: 'I'll do what I can, Lord Marchbrook. The moment I have anything to report, I'll get in touch with you.'

'Thank you, Mr. Granger.'

The earl brought out his wallet. He peeled off ten fifty-pound notes, laid them on the desk and said calmly: 'That is for current expenditure. If you are successful in recovering the necklace without scandal, I will pay you an additional ten thousand pounds.'

Granger felt — and looked — faint. The fee was fantastic. In a daze he escorted the earl to the door personally and wished him good day. Then he returned to the inner office and studied the notes he had made. Coming to a sudden decision, he rose, donned coat and hat, then paused as Miss Green's head appeared again.

'Viscount Sorbo wishes to see you, Mr. Granger,' she piped.

Granger sat down again weakly. 'How interesting! Please show him in, Miss Green. This certainly is a family party!'

2

Revelry by Night

Viscount Sorbo fully justified his distasteful reputation. His dissipated way of life showed in the half-circles under his mean eyes and in the cruel downstrokes running from the bridge of his nose to the ends of his lips, and more than ever in the thin gash of the lips themselves. His chin was weak and receding, his hair oily and black, and greying at the sides. In spite of the fact that he was only twenty-eight, he could easily have passed for a man of forty. He was almost foppishly attired, and carried an ebony cane.

Granger immediately disliked him, and the subsequent talk they had did little to alter this opinion. The viscount didn't mince his words; he came straight to the point.

'I believe my father called on you a short time ago in connection with a certain matter?'

'Do you?' said Granger warily. 'Well, what of it?'

'Did he or did he not?' said Sorbo irritably.

'Suppose I were to say he did not?' said Granger, goaded.

'Then I would say you were a liar!'

'Thank you. Since you appear to be fully satisfied that he did, why ask? If you have anything to discuss with me, kindly keep to the details and start at once. My time is valuable.'

Sorbo laughed. 'Valuable? You? A cheap private detective who makes his living spying on people, guarding cheap wedding trinkets, and snooping in divorce cases? Your time, valuable! My hat!'

'It's much more valuable than yours,' said Granger shortly. 'I have to earn my bread and butter the hard way. I don't lead a dissolute life on money which is given to me. I expect if your father put you to work for a living, it might teach you the value of money and also a few manners.'

Sorbo half-rose, anger glinting in his fishy eyes. He said: 'Why, you —! Do you think for one second you can insult me? Do you imagine I'll sit here and let myself be criticised by a third-rate detective?'

'The remedy is in your own hands. The office door is behind you. Good afternoon, Sorbo. Get out!'

Sorbo bit his lip and relaxed into the chair. 'I didn't come here to quarrel with you, Granger,' he said more calmly. 'I came to ask you to cooperate with me. If I was boorish, I apologise. Won't you listen for just a moment?'

'Well, make it short and snappy.'

'First of all, I don't want to put this too bluntly, but if you do as I ask, I'll pay you two thousand pounds here and now in cash.'

'Exactly what do you want me to do?'

Sorbo leaned back, laid his stick against the chair side, and put his fingertips together. For some moments he stared at the ceiling, and just as Granger was beginning to get impatient, he said: 'It isn't exactly a question of what I want you to do. It's rather a matter of what I *don't* want you to do, if you understand me. I'm willing to give you this money for doing exactly nothing.'

'I don't get you.'

'Well, my father was here, wasn't he? I know because I trailed him from the Towers in a taxi. I had an idea he'd contact some private detective. He as good as told me that. He wanted you to find Lesley Lyle for him. Isn't that right? Well, I will pay you two thousand pounds not to find her. Is that clear, Granger?'

Rodney Granger lit a cigarette and blew smoke towards the fop. 'Sorry, Sorbo. I can't accept your commission. I've already undertaken to find the woman, and I've accepted a retainer from your father.'

'Don't worry about Father's money. Keep it. Just pretend you've been working on the case but can't find anything out. Soak the old fool for as much as he will give you — but please don't take the case, and don't find the woman.'

'Why?'

Sorbo wriggled in his chair. 'I don't want Lesley caught. I'm rather fond of her, you see. If she's got the necklace, good luck to her. I can't say I blame her. Father and mother were rotten to her when she was introduced. Now do you see the motive?'

'No, I don't. Candidly, I can't picture you as a chivalrous man. It's like putting a figure by Picasso into a setting by Rembrandt — it doesn't fit. It doesn't harmonise. If you asked my opinion, I'd say chivalry and you were very far apart.'

'I don't ask your opinion,' grunted Sorbo. 'I offer you two thousand for stepping out of the picture. I want the woman to get away. What does it matter to you why? You can easily fool my father into believing you're working on the case. Let him pay and to blazes with him. He can afford to be swindled!'

Granger nodded and held out his hand. 'I see your point. Very well, Sorbo, I'll take the two thousand now.'

Sorbo looked relieved, stood up and delved into his pocket. The money was already made up into a neat elastic-banded bundle. He threw it on the desk and said: 'I'm glad you're sensible, Granger. Remember this is entirely in confidence.'

'I won't forget that.'

Rodney took the money, crossed to a wall safe, swung it open and placed the money inside. Then he shut the door and closed the combination with a spin. There was a peculiar smile on his face when he looked at Sorbo, who was preparing to leave.

'I think you're rather a fool, Sorbo. I guess drink has gone to your brain.'

Sorbo scowled. 'The fact that I have asked you to do this for me doesn't entitle you to abuse me, Mr. Granger.'

'But I'm simply stating the truth. You must be a fool to hand over two thousand pounds to a person without receipt or witnesses, now, mustn't you? Suppose, for instance, I had no intention of honouring our verbal agreement?'

Sorbo turned back from the door, furious. He gasped: 'Do you mean to say you would take that money and then fall down on your half of the bargain?'

'That's it,' said Granger cheerfully. 'I've no intention of being bought off. I'm still going to find that woman and the necklace.'

'You — you rogue! You damned swindler!' shouted Sorbo, livid with anger. 'I'll take you to court — I'll —'

'You'll do nothing at all in the matter. If you were so sure I'd be ready to swindle your father, how can you blame me for swindling you? Of course, if you insist, I'll call the police myself.'

He picked up the phone, and Sorbo snarled: 'You know I daren't let it be known that I paid you to stay off the case. But by heaven, Granger, you won't get away with it. I've got a way of dealing with your sort.'

The blow he aimed at the detective was feeble and badly timed. Granger had no difficulty in warding it off, and then his own fist smashed into the viscount's aristocratic nose, knocking him to the floor and drawing blood.

Sorbo howled and picked himself up weakly. He glared at Granger and said sullenly: 'I'll make you sorry you did that.'

Granger smiled sweetly after him as the viscount barged from the inner office, handkerchief to his nose. When the outer door slammed, Miss Green entered.

'What on *earth* are you doing, Mr. Granger?' she said blankly. 'What happened to that man's nose?'

'The viscount? Oh, just a slight example of someone sticking his nose too far into other people's business and getting it jammed. I'm sorry I had to spill his blue blood.'

'It didn't look blue to me,' sniffed Miss Green. 'Matter of fact, it looked more like water.'

'Miss Green! How unkind of you to say so. Viscount Sorbo is quite a prominent member of the peerage.'

'He's no gentleman, and I should say he was forward rather than prominent. He actually had the nerve to get fresh with me as he was coming into your office.'

Granger grinned. 'I thought you looked rather red when you announced him. But really, it should be counted a signal honour to be pinched by a viscount.'

'It may be to *some*,' said Miss Green dangerously, 'but not to me. If he ever comes back here and tries his tricks on me again, I'll make his head so sore he won't be able to wear his coronet for a week.'

'I don't think he'll trouble us again,' Granger told her. 'If I'm not mistaken, he's gone for good. Now, if I can ask a favour of you, your company tonight for a little excursion I'm planning would be invaluable. I'd like you to don your best rags and accompany me to a nest known as The

120

Sound of Revelry by Night. I'll explain your part in the affair when we get safely inside. What do you say?'

* * *

The Sound of Revelry by Night opened its doors as usual at six p.m. promptly that evening. It stood in a narrow side street, and had originally been a cinema of sorts. Until recently it had been derelict, and then had been bought by a Mr. Popolousilis, who, in spite of his Grecian title, hailed from no further afield than Bloomsbury. Nevertheless, he talked broken English every night at his club — quite unaware that his select patrons referred to him as 'Lousy'.

This particular night he was feeling happier than ever. The club didn't start its heavy business until ten or eleven. Then the theatregoers came in to take advantage of the British law which let them drink until midnight as long as they kept one stale sandwich or piece of cake at their table.

Meanwhile, Lousy opened his rear gambling room for the select few. The cause of his jubilation this particular evening was in the shape of a phone call from that depraved young man, Viscount Sorbo. The viscount owed much money to Lousy, and he had told the owner that he would be round to pay his debts that night. Accordingly, Lousy was delighted with everything, and confidently looked forward to seeing the viscount deprived of a great deal more than he already owed.

It was at nine o'clock, just as the place was beginning to fill up, that two strangers arrived. The doorman stopped them and told them courteously that the club was for members only. Could they produce cards? They couldn't? Hmm. He was afraid he couldn't let them in.

'Look here,' said the tall, black-haired young man, relaxing his grip upon the arm of his blonde, sophisticated companion. 'We simply have to get in, what? I mean, dash it all, we're expected — aren't we, old gel?'

'Oh, rather. Absolutely,' agreed his fair companion.

'Expected?' said the doorman. 'Who expects you, sir?'

'We're friends of Lord Sorbo, y'know. I am the Duke of Blunderbuss, and this is

Countess Gracias Senuras. Sorbo told us he'd see us here tonight.'

The doorman scratched his thick head and reflected. 'Lord Sorbo ain't arrived yet, yer grace. Likely he won't be 'ere until after eleven.'

'How dashed annoying,' said the Duke of Blunderbuss aggrievedly. 'But — couldn't we wait for him inside the jolly old club?'

'I don't know as 'ow ... Oh! Thankee, yer grace. Yes, I expect it'll be all right. Just go in, will you.' The doorman tucked the pound-note in his cap-band, and the duke and the countess passed inside.

'Simple,' said Granger with a smile. 'See what a little bribery and corruption does, my dear countess?'

Miss Green, minus her horn-rims, nodded.

'And if we don't find something out here,' Granger added, 'my name will be mud.'

3

Ladies Must Live

The fake Duke of Blunderbuss and Countess of Gracias Senuras were seized by a head waiter as they entered, and dragged to a front table. They looked and acted wealthy. Granger ordered drinks and waved away the dinner menu. They gazed about, apparently bored to death, but really weighing up the place keenly.

'I'm going over to the bar,' Granger told Miss Green. 'Stick around here and keep your eyes and ears open. If you hear anything of interest, come across and join me.'

She nodded, and he sauntered casually into the room with the arched door and found himself a niche at the long bar. He didn't see the three men whose tough faces betrayed their gentlemanly dress and who gazed at him curiously as he entered.

He ordered whisky straight. His attention, as he drank, was entirely taken by the woman on his left side, who was drinking alone, sipping her liquor with little delicate sips, and questing the bar with her wide, blue eyes. His memory stirred. He seemed to recall her features, but where and when could he have seen her? Wait a minute — yes! Society papers — photograph section — Lady Lossa Campton and friend! His vague thoughts crystallised into certainties.

Granger tapped her gently on the arm and said: 'How do you do, Lady Lossa? You'll forgive me for renewing our acquaintanceship in this manner.'

She turned to look at him. 'I don't think we have ever met, have we?'

He smiled. 'No, I admit we haven't. Not socially. But I've seen quite a lot of you in the picture papers. It's rather novel to meet you in the … hmm!'

'The flesh?' she said, allowing her eyes to roam over him quizzically. 'I hope you aren't disappointed!'

His eyes wandered over her in turn, so casually that the rudeness wasn't apparent. He took in the carefully fixed hair of a glossy auburn tint, and the greenish-blue eyes; the green was not visible until you looked deep into them. It lurked behind the blue and amazed you by its presence there. Her nose was finely shaped, an adorable little nose. Her lips were full, red and kissable; and if there were tiny lines at the corners of her eyes, what of it? Her slim figure to which the stuff of her gown clung more than made up for these signs of a hectic life. A small pulse in her throat throbbed intoxicatingly.

He said: 'I'm delighted. I had thought your photographs flattered you — now I see they don't even do you justice.'

'Thank you, er —?'

'Stern. My name is Stern, Joseph Stern,' he invented. 'I'm over here on a visit from my native country — Canada.'

'Mr. Stern. Now that the formalities are completed, may I ask you how you like London?'

'Not bad,' he admitted. 'But it can't match up to Ontario. There isn't a touch of freedom here.'

'In what way?' she asked inquisitively.

'I don't know exactly, but back home I was always able to get a game of some description or other when I wanted. Over here the police seem tighter on the gambling saloons.'

He had hoped this would prompt her to reveal something of value about the hidden attractions which the club had to offer, but she didn't take the cue. Either she didn't know about the gambling rooms, or she was cautious to whom she spoke. She laughed and said: 'I suppose you're quite a big gambler? Most of you people from over there are, aren't you?'

'Well, personally, I do play for pretty high stakes,' he admitted. 'I don't suppose you could take me anywhere where I might get a game? Or recommend me to someone who might know?'

'I really couldn't recommend you to anyone yet. I don't know you very well, do I? Suppose you buy me a drink now, and we'll talk about gambling later.'

'Right! What will you have?'

'Pink Lady, please.'

She didn't speak again until the drink was brought. Then she said: 'How did you get in here, Mr. Stern? I mean, this is a private club, and if you came from Canada only recently, I can't quite see how you got a membership card.'

'I happen to have a warm acquaintance with Viscount Sorbo — very warm,' he added, thinking of the events of the afternoon. 'His magic name worked the oracle. I'm waiting for him now, by the way.'

She looked at him closely with an expression in her eyes which he failed to read. 'Aren't you a great deal too early if you're waiting for him? He seldom turns up until after eleven.'

'I suppose I am. But I thought I might as well wait here as anywhere.'

She sipped her cocktail and studied the crimson polish on her fingernails. Suddenly she smiled at him and said frankly: 'If you really do want a game of roulette, I might arrange things for you. You see, we do have gaming rooms here.'

'You do? You've played here?'

She smiled at him and said: 'I'm afraid I'm odd, Mr. Stern, but I detest any kind of gambling.'

'But —'

'How do I know about the gambling here? Is that what you're wondering? How can I make it all right for you to join the game? Simple. I'll let you into a secret, Mr. Stern. I work here as a glorified hostess. It's my job to weigh up each prospective player, and signify my approval or otherwise. I know most of the people who use this place; they're from my own set. I can usually tell whether they're trustworthy and good losers.'

'Mercy! You certainly are an amazing woman.'

'Because I work here? Lossa Campton working as hostess in a gambling saloon! Yes, I expect it is rather surprising, but a woman has to live — even so-called ladies must eat sometimes, Mr. Stern, and I have quite an unfeminine appetite. Besides, I get paid well, and I prefer this work to taking a post as governess or welfare superintendent, which is usually the fate of overbred women without incomes.'

'I understand now. Of course, if you're broke, that explains things.'

'Broke is right. The funds in the family chest are so low you have to bend double even to scoop out one doubloon. And since I'm not a snobbish person, nor a person who suffers from an exalted idea of her position — since I am, in fact, a thoroughly worthless member of society — I have no scruples about the way I make money. I have other methods besides being a hostess.'

'This is fascinating. Go on.'

'Well, I sometimes act as a paid escort. For a reasonable sum I'm ready to lend 'tone' to any party. I've been the paid date of scores of men.'

Granger leaned forward tensely. 'Including wolves?'

'Now you're being indiscreet!' She took a big gulp of cocktail. 'Yes, sometimes they are wolves with long fangs. I remember one middle-aged banker — but there, that isn't a story I could safely tell to a young man. It isn't even for the smoking room of a men's club. Ah well, on the whole, I manage admirably. I have a knack of being able to take good care of myself. Men, for instance, hate to have lighted cigarettes pressed on their hands.'

Granger smiled. 'Thanks for the warning. I'll remember that.'

'Will you?' She looked at him enigmatically again, sighed and drained her drink.

'You know, men do make the most absolute fools of themselves at times. They're like a baby with a lollipop — positively maudlin when they're thwarted. You wouldn't be so utterly foolish as that, would you, Mr. Stern?'

'I don't know. I might be. You're enough to turn anyone's head.'

'How sweet of you. But didn't I see you come in with a partner?'

'Did you? Oh yes. She's my secretary. I brought her along for a treat.'

'Hmm. Quite a secretary! Tell me, Mr. Stern, does she really know shorthand and typing?'

Granger laughed. They had another drink, then she said: 'Will you excuse me a moment while I see if I can smuggle you into the gaming rooms?'

'Certainly.' He watched her walk across the bar towards a small door at the far end. He waited patiently. After ten minutes he wandered to the dance floor, bought half a dozen tickets at the kiosk, nodded distantly to Miss Green, who stared at him outraged, and walked across to the line of taxi dancers.

He chose the end woman. She was the youngest, scarcely older than twenty-one. She had black hair which she wore in a loose style, and liquid brown eyes. She looked young and innocent, and made a great contrast to her hard-bitten companions. Granger decided she would be most likely to be fooled into talking about the missing singer. When he handed her his ticket she got to her feet nervously. They drifted over the floor, which was getting crowded, and he said: 'I like the band you have here.'

'The band? Oh, yes. They are rather good. Lousy — I mean Mr. Popolousilis — chose them carefully; they're all top men on their own instruments.'

'Mr. Popolousilis? Is he the proprietor?'

'Yes. Everyone calls him Lousy here, but actually that's only a nickname. He has a fine, big heart.'

Granger nodded. 'By the way, some friends of mine once mentioned a singer to me. They said she worked here; a Lesley Lyle, I think the name was. I haven't heard her yet. Is she still with the band?'

The effect of his words was startling;

the woman glanced up at him, her eyes opening with alarm. She whispered: 'I'm sorry. I can't remember anyone of that name working here. I — I haven't been here long myself.'

'Never mind. I only asked because these friends told me she had a very distinctive style.'

The music stopped, and she began to walk back towards the line. He laid a detaining hand on her shoulder and said: 'Please! I've still got five tickets. I'd like to dance them all with you.'

'But — but it isn't really fair on the other women, is it?'

'Perhaps not. But I'm afraid I'm not gallant. If I were to dance with them, I'd feel I'd been cheated out of my money. Honestly, I'd much rather dance with you. There aren't any rules against it, are there?'

'Well, no.' But she seemed anxious to get away from him after that one leading question. They drifted off again to the strains of a slow foxtrot and the crooning of the slender young man with the bow-tie and the agonised expression.

They had circled towards the entrance of

the club when suddenly the woman's eyes became fixed, staring magnetically over Granger's shoulder. She stared for seconds only; then she twisted her face round so that he had to guide her until she was dancing with her back to the door. Granger saw the cause for her alarm. Lord Sorbo, sporting a badly swollen nose, had just entered!

Granger, too, didn't want to be seen by the man, so at once he performed a double-reverse which carried them into the thick of the dancers. The music stopped again, and the dancers clapped listlessly and stood about, waiting for the second encore.

The woman gasped: 'Please excuse me. I must leave you for a moment.' Thrusting the remaining tickets back into his hand, she pushed through the crowd towards a door marked 'Ladies' Cloakroom'.

Granger stared after her for a moment. Then he went back to the table at which Miss Green sat. She said at once: 'Sorbo's here.'

'I know. I've seen him.'

'And he's seen you,' went on Miss Green. 'While you were so busy with your conquests, I noticed him looking you up and down. Look out for trouble!'

'Don't be ridiculous, Miss Green. What trouble could possibly happen inside a semi-respectable and crowded club?'

'I don't know. But if he has friends, and they could get you alone, plenty could, I guess.'

'They won't get me alone. I'll take care of that. Another drink, my dear Countess?' he added as an immaculate waiter floated past.

Miss Green nodded. 'I don't mind if I do, my dear Duke.'

When the waiter left to get the drinks, she hissed: 'Wasn't that Lady Lossa Campton you were talking to at the bar?'

'It was — and guess what, my dear Countess — she works here as a hostess!'

'I'm not surprised. What else were you two talking about, my dear Duke? Or am I too innocent to know?'

'I doubt that, but I admit that we talked of fur coats, among other things, such as —'

Miss Green raised her hand in a pained manner. 'Stop! Spare me the embarrassing details.'

'There aren't any. Our conversation wouldn't have offended a bishop — well, perhaps it would, but I expect it would have got by a school mistress without trouble.'

'Knowing one or two school mistresses in particular, I daresay it would,' agreed Miss Green cattily. 'Look out. Here she comes now.'

Lady Lossa had walked across and bent seductively over Granger's left shoulder. She said: 'If you'd care to join the tables now, I've arranged it.'

He got up and walked after her. Miss Green whispered maliciously after him: 'Mind you don't lose your boiled shirt, dear Duke. Remember, it's hired!'

4

Unsavoury Company

Lady Lossa led him through the long bar to the end of the room and towards the baize door. The gambling room was immediately behind this. Men and women in evening dress were gathered round the green tables, tense with the eager feverishness of inveterate gamblers. Suave croupiers spun the wheel and called the numbers; polished bank-men threw dice on other tables. At a small office a woman gave out chips pertly.

'You were rather a long time,' Granger told Lady Lossa as he changed a fifty-pound note for a stack of blues. 'I'd begun to think they weren't letting me in after all.'

She said: 'Lousy wasn't going to at first. He said it was too risky. But a few moments ago I noticed him having a word with Viscount Sorbo, and then he came and told me to bring you along.'

An electric thrill tremored along

Granger's spine — a current of fierce warning of dangers ahead. He noticed Viscount Sorbo staring at him malignantly from a small bar at the end of the room. Sorbo was talking to a short stout man, who nodded every now and then.

Carefully ignoring them, Granger crossed to the roulette table and jostled a place for himself. Across from him, he caught the eye of a thin, cadaverous-looking man with piercing grey eyes. It was 'Barter' Brand, the most noted fence in London.

Brand, of course, didn't recognise such a small-time private dick as Granger, but the detective spotted the fence. He fitted the description. Granger guessed that many crooks must infest the place, rubbing elbows with socialites, and uncovering invaluable information for blackmail, breaking and entering, and other unsavoury jobs. Granger laid ten pounds on number three, watched the croupier spin the wheel, and glared, fascinated, at the bouncing ball.

'Number three,' sang out the croupier, and his rake scooped up the chips and pushed them across the table towards

Granger. Granger laid fifty pounds in chips on number seven. The wheel spun.

Three men who had been drinking in the long bar previously suddenly clustered round him. One of them tapped him on the shoulder and said softly: 'Come on quietly. You're wanted outside.'

Granger went very cool, as he always did when trouble was near. 'Am I? Just hang on until this spin is finished, will you?'

The croupier sang out: 'Number seven.'

Granger gathered up his winnings and turned regretfully to the three tough guys behind him. 'Now I can deal with you gentlemen. What exactly is it you want?'

'Someone wants to see you. Don't start any trouble.'

'I don't intend to,' he told them with a lazy smile. 'You boys just toddle along and forget all about me. Tell Sorbo that if he wants to see me, he'll find me here. Otherwise it's no go. Get it?'

An ugly specimen with the beetling brow of a bruiser thrust his ugly face at Granger and breathed foul air over him. 'So you wanta be tough about it?'

'Not at all, but I hardly see what you can

do to make me come along if I don't want to.'

He glanced significantly towards the other players who were leaning over the table excitedly. So far they had not heard any of the menacing conversation, but it was clearly impossible for the three thugs forcibly to eject Granger. The private detective was counting on this.

He was mistaken; the men had been quite prepared for toughness. The beetle -browed one stepped forward suddenly, and before Granger knew what was coming, swung a punch at his jaw. It was a punch which would have given Joe Louis a lot to think about, but it didn't give Granger much time for thought. It just removed his capacity for philosophy entirely. He flopped ungracefully to the floor. The startled roulette players craned round in amazement.

'I say; someone's been slugged,' said a woman who was a baroness.

'All right, folks,' called out one of the thugs without batting an eyelid. 'The man had too much to drink. He just passed out. We'll attend to him.'

'Here, hold on,' interjected a

timid-looking player. 'He didn't go out through drink. The big chap hit him. I saw it.'

'You what, mister?' said the beetle-browed hulk, his eyes two stony gimlets.

The timid man recoiled from the look and said: 'I mean I thought — that is — my eyes are rather weak,' he explained apologetically. 'Perhaps I was mistaken.'

'You oughtn't to say things like that,' said Beetle-brow, pained. 'You might get into trouble someday.'

Without further objections, the three hoisted the senseless Granger onto their shoulders and marched unconcernedly towards a rear door. The proprietor joined them, and they passed into what had originally been a dressing-room, but which was now well-appointed as an office. Viscount Sorbo was waiting there, and when he saw the unconscious man he chuckled delightedly.

They tied Granger quickly to a chair by his legs and wrists. Then Lousy slapped water over him with a wet cloth until his eyes blinked wearily open. His gaze met Sorbo's, and he gave a slight grin at the sight of the other man's red and swollen nose. He said: 'Hello, Sorbo. I hadn't any idea you were so anxious to see me. How's the boko?'

Sorbo scowled and ran a tender finger along his nose. 'I'd advise you to save your humour until you're sure it will be appreciated, Granger. It's quite out of place here.'

'Let me talk to him,' said Lousy, discarding his Greek accent for the moment. Sorbo looked reluctant, but stepped back obediently. The stout, heavily jewelled man came over and stood in front of Granger. 'We don't want to hurt you, mister. We brought you here to give a warning. You are not to interfere in the Lesley Lyle case. Do you understand?'

'So you're in it, too?' echoed Granger. 'Hmm. She is about here somewhere, then?'

'No. But even if she was, it's none of your business. We want your word to leave the case alone. You walked in here claiming a friendship with Sorbo so as you could snoop. Well, you found out nothing, and you won't. But if you want to stay healthy, mind your own confounded business.'

'And if I don't?'

'I'm warning you; unless you give us your word and keep it, we'll get nasty.'

'Why waste time?' Viscount Sorbo said. 'We'd better give him a practical demonstration.' He stepped forward again, holding his lighted cigarette in his fingers, his face a mask of gloating.

Lousy snapped: 'No, my lord! We aren't doing anything like that. Not until we have to. Maybe he'll be content to lay off now.'

'I'm sorry, gents,' said Granger. 'I must make a living, mustn't I?'

'You see!' Sorbo snapped. 'It isn't any use talking. Let me handle him a minute. I owe him something for this nose.'

'I think it's rather an improvement,' said Granger admiringly. 'Much better than the old model.'

Lousy and his thugs smiled, but stepped aside and nodded to the wrathful viscount. Lousy said: 'He's a bit fresh. Maybe a tap or two wouldn't hurt him any.'

Sorbo almost purred with sadistic gloating. He stood almost on top of Granger and rasped: 'I told you I'd get even. How would you like your nose putting in this shape? How do you like this, Granger?'

He shot his fist forward, and it smashed home on Granger's nose. Blood spurted, and Granger winced as Sorbo drew back his fist again. Lousy said: 'Now will you agree to forget all about Lesley Lyle?'

'Not a bit,' Granger returned. 'I'm more determined than ever, old top.'

'You're damned obstinate. All right, give him another, Viscount.'

Sorbo grinned wickedly, bunched his fist and stooped down. His intention was obvious. He meant to punch the bound man violently in the stomach, but it didn't work out that way.

As he bent, Granger lurched himself forward and the top of his head cracked sickeningly against Sorbo's face. The depraved peer staggered back with a wild yell, clutching his unfortunate nose, which had sustained the brunt of the knock. He roared with pain.

Lousy said: 'Stop making that noise, my lord. The people in there will hear.'

'But my nose — my nose —!' howled Sorbo.

Granger said: 'I'm sorry about your snout, Sorbo. Honestly, I meant to try and butt you on the chin, but just missed. Really, I wouldn't have altered the shape of your beak for a fortune. But you do rather insist on sticking it out, don't you, old man?'

Sorbo looked murderous. He grated: 'There's only one way to deal with this damned meddling swine. We'll castor-oil him.'

'No. We're not going that far,' said Lousy with a great deal of haste. 'I think he's had his lesson. We'll turn him free now, and if he butts in again he knows what he'll get.'

Granger was hastily pulled from the chair and untied. He mopped blood from his nose and chin and flexed his aching limbs.

Lousy said: 'We don't intend you to find that woman, Granger. We'll go to any lengths eventually, if you haven't the sense to the leave the case alone.'

'But now I'm free, eh?'

'That's the idea. You see, we figure your lady-friend may get inquisitive about you. We'll let you out by the back door, and get the waiter to tell her you're waiting for her outside.'

'You aren't afraid I'll go to the police?'

'I don't think you will. According to Viscount Sorbo here, the Earl of Marchbrook wants this case done privately. And if you do report, his lordship is quite willing to testify he was in this room all night, and will say you were brought in here drunk, revived, and thrown out the back way, probably bumping your nose against the step as you went.'

'You win, gentlemen,' said Granger with a smile. 'I won't report this, but only for one solitary reason.'

'Which is?'

'Because I don't want this place closed down. You see, I believe the missing woman is here somewhere. I don't know what hand you have in the game, and I don't know where Viscount Sorbo comes into it, either, but I'll find out.'

'The day you do, Mr. Granger, will be a most unfortunate day for you. Show him the door, boys.'

Lousy crossed the room and opened a door which led to the gaming-room. Beyond this was a straight, short corridor, and at its end was a double door with a pushbar. Granger took in all this mechanically, and turned again to face Lord Sorbo. He said: 'I don't like you, Sorbo. Nor do I like the way you seem to be interested in this case. That last knock you had has put your nose almost back to normal — and that isn't good, either. Perhaps this will remedy things.'

Before anyone could guess his intention, Granger's upswept knuckles smacked home into Sorbo's long-suffering nose. Then, as the viscount staggered back with a thin yell, Granger ducked past the astonished thugs, and Lousy called a mocking good night and thrust his weight against the pushbar.

Then Granger found himself in the open, and began running swiftly down the road towards the front of the club. He hailed a passing taxi, climbed in, and told the driver to wait near to the club door with the engine running.

It wasn't long before Miss Green wandered out looking slightly overwhelmed. She stood on the pavement undecidedly. Granger pushed open the cab door and called: 'Haven't we met before, my dear Countess?'

She peered at him, then climbed into the cab beside him. She sniffed: 'Have we? I'm sure I don't know anyone with a nose like that. What on earth has been happening to you, you idiot?'

'The dear viscount wanted to make sure I had red blood in my veins. I also massaged his proboscis for him again. Twice, actually. Let's hope he'll need the services of a bone-setter after this.'

She smiled. 'How did you get out?'

'Through the back way — probably because dear old Lousy didn't want his customers to see me looking mangled.' He settled lower in the upholstery. 'What do you know, Countess?'

'Not much. There was only one thing: just after you'd gone, Viscount Sorbo came back to the club, holding his nose in a handkerchief. He went straight up to the woman you danced with. She'd come out of the ladies' room by then and was in the taxi dancers' line again. Well, she started to get up as he came across. It seemed she wanted to dodge him. But she was too late. He began talking to her, and before long she was actually giving him a grateful look. They were still talking when a pug-ugly tough came up to me and told me my escort was waiting outside. I got the feeling I wasn't wanted, so I went, and here I am.'

Granger scratched his head. 'So Sorbo buttonholed that woman? I wonder just what she knows about all this. I'm sure she knows something.'

'I shouldn't be surprised. She looks too innocent to be true. But you won't be able to get in touch now, will you? You can't go back to that club again unless you like having your nose atomised.'

'Frankly, I don't. But what's one nose compared to ten thousand pounds, which is mine if the job is pulled off?'

'Ten thousand?' Miss Green gave him a haughty stare. 'So it's as much as that, is it? And I expect you'd give me a measly five pounds as my bonus, wouldn't you?'

'No, no. I fully intend you to have at least five hundred if all goes well.'

'See you do; and while you're moving among the big money, you can also raise my paltry salary.'

'Your salary? Er — what do you get now?'

'You know very well what I get. A niggardly four pounds a week. I'll want at least seven if I'm going to help you with this job.

Don't forget I'm being married shortly. I'll have a husband to support.'

He grinned. 'All right. Yon shall have your raise if I earn that fee. Don't worry; perhaps I might get your husband a job cleaning out the office, too. Doesn't he earn *any* money of his own?'

'Not a penny,' sighed Miss Green. 'He's a poet!'

'Ye gods!' Granger groaned, and dropped the subject. He also dropped Miss Green — at her flat, and went on in the cab to his own rooms. It had been a wearing day — too wearing for him to see Sandra Lyle reclining on his settee when he entered his rooms — but that was exactly what he did see!

She was looking dangerously alluring.

5

A Lady Visits Late at Night!

Reactions to the discovery of a beautiful young lady in a man's rooms late at night vary according to the discoverer, in the normal course of events. Rodney, being as Miss Green had alleged, a 'wolf', would have greeted the discovery almost as enthusiastically as did Columbus when the New World hove into view. But tonight his outlook was different.

Rodney Granger had had a very wearing and trying day. He was tired, and his head and chin ached from the attentions of the tough with the beetling brows; his nose was swollen and sore, and although he had the satisfaction of knowing that Viscount Sorbo's would be — as it were — swollener and sorer, he still wanted peace and solitude while he attended to his injury, and then all he asked for was a good night's sleep.

Accordingly, he did not greet the

woman's presence with glad cries and hungry barks. Instead he gave her an irritated look and said: 'Well, Miss Lyle, how on earth did you get in here?'

'Please don't be angry with me, Mr. Granger. I just walked in. You weren't at home, and the door was unlocked, so I thought I'd wait for you. I've been here about three quarters of an hour. I found some magazines to glance through, but they weren't quite my type.' She indicated a pile of *La Vie Parisienne* on an occasional table, and Rodney had the grace to look confused.

'But what brought you so late?' he said to change the subject. 'I told you I'd do all I could to help. I'll let you know when I get results.'

She delved into her handbag and drew out a sheet of notepaper. 'But what about this? One of the staff from The Sound of Revelry by Night brought it to me tonight, about ten o'clock. I thought you ought to see it.'

He read:

Sandra, darling,

I know you must be awfully worried about the way I left today while you were making late breakfast. But when I read the eleven o'clock edition of the paper, I was afraid, and I'll tell you why.

You'll soon know that the police suspected me of stealing the Marchbrook necklace. I needn't tell you that I didn't steal it, but the circumstances surrounding my leaving the Towers all pointed to me as the thief. Yet, believe me, Sandra dear, I didn't even know the thing was missing until I read that paper. Then I took fright and decided to go into hiding. I didn't wait for explanations. That would have taken too long.

Now I feel you must be very worried; the police must have been to see you by now, and I know just how rotten it must be for you. I'd like to see you and explain. If you could meet me at the address I give below tomorrow, I'd be awfully grateful. I'll take a room for the afternoon in the name of Sheila Allen, and I'll wait for you from four to five there. Don't reveal the contents of this note to anyone, and please do come.

Your worried and loving sister, Lesley.

Granger looked up quickly. 'You say one of the staff of the club brought this?'

'Yes; Maudie, the cloak-room attendant.'

Granger nodded and gave her the note back. 'What do you intend to do about it?'

'That's exactly what I came to see *you* about. I don't really know how to advise her for the best. But you can help me, Mr. Granger.'

'I'm afraid my advice would be for your sister to give herself up to the police. The evidence is very damning, but I feel sure her innocence will be proved sooner or later. Yet suppose, for argument's sake, she did steal the necklace — well, I know Lord Marchbrook wouldn't prosecute if she returned it. But if she didn't, she couldn't very well return it, could she? And, of course, he'd probably think she'd disposed of it, and he would prosecute. It's rather awkward all round.'

'It's awful!' Sandra twisted her hands together. 'Then you advise me to see her and tell her to give herself up?'

'Definitely. At once. The police will find her sooner or later, you know. They aren't such fools as popular novels make out. Lesley should come clean. It's the only way.'

'I think you're right. Then I'll tell her to

make a clean breast of it, shall I?'

'Do. And let me know what she decides before she actually does give herself up, will you? Now, if you'll take the address she gave you and then burn that note, it would be safer.'

She nodded and tore off the address, which was of a hotel in the Bayswater Road. She put the rest of the note in the ashtray and touched a match to it. Then she surveyed Granger's swollen eye critically.

'Your eye's in an awful state, Mr. Granger,' she said sympathetically. 'It's going to be a shocking colour tomorrow.'

'I know. I ran into a door,' he said nonconmittally.

She smiled. 'That's what they all say. Mind if I fix it for you? I'm rather an expert on bodies and things. I took my St. John's last year.'

'Oh, don't bother, Miss Lyle. A good night's sleep will fix it, plus a slab of beefsteak when the butcher opens.'

But her lovely mouth tightened in a business-like way and she began to strip off her gloves and coat. 'I insist on fixing it now. Just sit on the settee. Is this the bathroom?

I must have water.'

She vanished, and he heard the sound of running water. She was back inside a minute with a bowl and some bottles from the medicine chest. He lay back while her cool hands worked on his injury, and he studied her serious features as she bent over him, engrossed in her work.

'There!' she said at last, stepping back and surveying him with a judicial eye. 'It looks better already.'

'It is better already,' he told her, sitting up. His tone was wicked. 'Thanks, nurse. Now do you suppose you could do anything to soothe my nerves?'

'Yes, I'll make a cup of coffee. Just relax and I'll have it ready in a moment.'

He gazed after her neat figure as she left the room and sighed. Now that his eye was more comfortable, he felt more like himself. He awaited her return with impatience.

Over the delicious coffee she had made, he told her briefly of the night's happenings; and although he glossed over the events in which he had played a fighting part, she was gazing at him admiringly when he concluded.

'So you actually got that eye in my interest?' she said.

'In a way, yes. But I ought to mention that I've also been retained by the Earl of Marchbrook to find your sister!'

She sat bolt upright. '*What!*'

'Don't worry,' he reassured her. 'I won't double-cross you. I'm not going to work on his side of the case for a while. The main job is to prove your sister is innocent. That's what I'm concentrating on now. By the way, did you know that Viscount Sorbo also tried to retain me?'

'He did? Why on earth would both he and his father want you?'

'That's the funny part of it all. Sorbo wanted me to stop the case; not to find your sister. He said if she had the necklace, good luck to her. She was welcome to it.'

'Sorbo said that? I can't believe it. That necklace was part of his inheritance. Why should he want Lesley to get away with it? Unless, of course, he really does love her.'

'No, I don't think it's that. There's something very odd about friend Sorbo. We must keep our eagle eye open. More coffee?'

She poured him a cup and said softly: 'I don't know how to thank you, Mr. Granger. You're giving me preference over all those important people. How can I ever repay you?'

Granger tried to control the naughty twinkle in his eye. 'You can show your gratitude by calling me Roddy, Sandra,' he told her. 'And don't worry yourself about my fee. Money isn't everything, and take my word that I enjoy doing this for you more than I would if I were doing it for Sorbo or his father, no matter how much I got out of it. All the earl's money can't buy him a well-turned ankle or a pretty face — and that's what appeals to me most.'

She thought for a moment and decided not to be alarmed. 'You really must be a wolf,' she said lightly.

'Right first time. According to Miss Green, I'm the biggest wolf outside the Siberian wastes.'

Sandra was deliberately casual as she asked: 'Who's Miss Green?'

'My secretary. And,' he added, 'she's very much engaged.'

'To you?'

'Mercy, no. To a poet, as a matter of fact. I can't quite understand how she could have fallen for a poet when I'm around every day, but such is fate.'

'Perhaps she knows you too well,' suggested Sandra. 'I should imagine you're an awfully bad type — horribly dangerous to women.'

He grinned ruefully. 'I asked for that. Seriously, though, I'm not quite as bad as I must have made you think. I do admire beauty in a woman, I admit. But I don't actually prowl the undergrowth looking for them.'

'I'm sure you don't, Mr. Granger — I mean, Roddy. If the truth were known, I expect you're really a babe in arms.' She gave him a tender smile that made his heart thump. Then she rose and he helped her on with her coat. 'I'll see Lesley tomorrow,' she said, 'and let you know how she decides. But suppose she thinks she's safer in hiding? What then?'

'Then we'll simply have to do our best to prove her innocence if we possibly can,' he told her. 'By the way, before you go to that address tomorrow, make absolutely sure you aren't followed by coveys of flat-footed gentlemen in bowler hats. If you are, go in the front, phone from the lobby for a taxi to meet you at the side entrance, and go out that way. Flop into the taxi, and you'll lose anyone who's shadowing you. There won't be another taxi handy near the side entrance. I know; I've used that dodge myself. It never fails.'

He saw her to the door and, in the corridor, she turned and gazed into his eyes. She said in her straightforward way: 'Why are you so decent about helping my sister and me when you know you could catch Lesley tomorrow and get the earl's fee?'

He scratched his head. 'I don't know. It's got me beat.'

'Would you have done it for any reasonably pretty woman?'

'No, I'm blessed if I would.' He grinned boyishly. 'Let's skip it, shall we?'

Then, to his surprise, she suddenly leaned forward and kissed him. He was still in a daze when she reached the stairs, waved, and vanished.

* * *

'It's damned awkward,' said Granger moodily. 'I hate hanging round waiting to see what happens when Sandra meets this sister of hers tonight. I'd like to do something more to help her.'

Miss Green said: 'Oh! It's *Sandra* now, is it? You wolf, you!'

'Not this time,' he said seriously. His tone went dreamy. 'I wondered what it was that attracted me to that woman. Now I know. I knew when we kissed last night. It was something completely magnetic.'

'Please,' begged Miss Green, giving him a stern glance through her spectacles. 'Remember I am but a young woman, Mr. Granger. Where did you kiss her?'

'On the lips,' said Granger, pleasantly reminiscent.

'I mean *where?* At what *location?*'

'My apartments, if it's any of your business, which it isn't. I'm not in the habit of asking you where your poet kisses you, am I?'

'I don't mind telling you: he invariably kisses me on the forehead. He says the lips are too mundane for such an ethereal love as ours.'

'Ye gods!' groaned Granger. 'You must have fun.'

'Don't worry,' said Miss Green determinedly. 'I'll alter him after we're married. I guarantee, too, that he'll have a job within a few weeks at the most. I'll make a new man of him.'

'You will? I must offer him my condolences,' said Granger.

'That's quite enough, Mr. Granger. You're just jealous. You know, sometimes I've been sorry I didn't hook you. I could have made a new man of you, too.'

'Heaven forbid!' said Granger feelingly. 'I'm happy as I am, thank you.'

'I know. Pigs invariably like groveling in dirt,' she said cattily. 'If you've nothing better to do than make cracks, why not slip along and see Nathan Gideon?'

Granger snapped his fingers. 'Why didn't I think of that myself? I'll go right now.'

He put on hat and coat and left the office, taking with him a roll of pound-notes from the safe. He scorned the buses and taxis, and walked leisurely through the traffic towards the junk market.

Among the vast, noisy, gesticulating throng of vendors, Nathan Gideon sold old junk in his own inimitable style. He was a landmark of the market; his customers were always sure of a good laugh from him. He had his own method of salesmanship, and was a picturesque character with his immense gold watch chain, his vital, oily face, and his battered black bowler.

He was also a mine of information. How he got it, no one quite knew, but get it he did. Someone had once hazarded that Nathan must have half the tramps in London working for him, and this seemed the most likely solution. Certainly he had a fund of knowledge on the doings of anyone in the public eye, and for a price he was always willing to compile a life history of anyone.

Granger found him at his usual stall, about to dispose of a large rolled-gold watch he was holding forth to the grinning spectators. 'The gent says it don't go. All right, so it don't go. What of it? Where else would you get a rolled-gold watch what doesn't go for half a dollar? It only needs adjustments. It's a handy thing; you can set it at ten o'clock, and then when you sneak in late and the wife wakes up, you could always show her it. That's the beauty of this watch. The damn thing ticks — but the hands don't move. I know a young woman who says men should be more like that. They should tick but ... well, you know the rest. Come on, come on, step up closer, don't be afraid; nobody's going to force you into anything. A few repairs will make this watch as good as new. Listen: this watch belonged to the Prime Minister of Oolongo. It's by way of being a family heirloom. You don't get bargains like this every day, you know. You could have it framed and hung in the front parlour. There's a history to it. Look — step up and see for yourselves — it's engraved, see? What's it say? Oh! 'Made in Germany', eh? All right, folks — sixpence. Who'll give me a 'tanner' for it? I ... Oh, hello there, Mr. Granger!'

He stopped his tirade and left the stall to his assistant as he noticed the private detective beckoning to him. He moved to a quieter corner with Granger and said: 'Haven't seen you for a long time, Mr. Granger. What brings yon along?'

'I'd like some information,' Granger told him.

'Another divorce case?'

'Not this time. I want a file on Lord Sorbo, with all the usual details of exactly what he's been up to in the last two months. And I want a file on a woman who used to sing at The Sound of Revelry by Night. Lesley Lyle, the name is. I want to know where she is now and what she's doing. But the most important thing is that I want to know where the Marchbrook necklace is; and if it's already in the hands of a fence, which one.'

Nathan pursed his thick lips and said: 'That'll be awkward, Mr. G. I don't know if I can find that out, and even if I did — well, I meantersay — you're not narking for the coppers, are you?'

'Nathan! You know me better than that. The information's for my own use. I won't mention how I came by it.'

'Well, I'll try. I got a source of information in the 'hot ice' game; maybe he'll know. But it'll cost plenty, Mr. Granger.'

'How much?'

'I can't say right off; but round about a

hundred quid all told.'

Granger handed him fifty and said: 'That's the usual retainer, Nathan. You get the rest after I get the 'dope.' O.K.?'

The other man nodded and stuffed the cash into a pouch strapped round his waist. 'I'll start the lads tracking down information right now, Mr. G. You'll have my report by tonight. The item that's going to be so expensive for you is that information about who's got the necklace. But if I don't find out for you, I'll make the fee straight. Trust me.'

Granger, as he walked back to his office, knew that every item of information he had requested would soon be in the process of being tracked down. Nathan had innumerable stooges on his payroll.

He spent a boring afternoon and left for home early. At ten past seven there was a knock, and he opened the door to Sandra, who looked remarkably happy.

She said: 'Lesley thinks as we do. She's going to give herself up! She says she's got nothing to lose. Can I come in? Or is the wolf biting today?'

6

Don't Play With Fire

'Sit down,' he invited her. 'Tell me about it.'

He mixed drinks and handed her one. She said: 'I kept the appointment. Though at first I thought I'd got into the wrong room. You see, Lesley's dyed her hair black.'

'Smart woman,' conceded Granger.

'It's surprising what a difference it makes. Anyone who knew her well could tell, of course, but anyone who happened to be looking for a blonde woman wouldn't connect. She told me the whole story. It was just as I had thought: she said that when she arrived at the Towers, Viscount Sorbo's parents were very cold and aloof. It didn't take her a minute to know she wasn't wanted. She'd have left then and there, because the whole snobbish crowd was getting on her nerves, but Sorbo persuaded her to stay when she spoke to him about it. He said she was to ignore them, that they were a lot of old fools, and as long as he wanted her there, what did anyone else matter?'

'So she stayed?'

'Yes; she decided she wouldn't give them the satisfaction of driving her away. She went to bed early, leaving Sorbo with the others in the smoking room.

'She said she couldn't sleep; and at about two o'clock, while she was lying there, staring into darkness, she heard her door opened quietly, and someone came into the room. At first she thought it was burglars. Then she realised that was hardly likely, since the earl had been holding forth to his guests on the invulnerability of his home, and the system of alarms he'd had installed. She then thought someone had gone into the wrong room by mistake, and she called out, asking who was there.

'Lord Sorbo's voice answered her! He told her to be quiet, not to make a row. He switched the lights on, and he had on only pajamas and a dressing-gown. She wasn't horrified. There's nothing Victorian about her. She thought he'd come along to have a chat and try to cheer her up about the rotten way she'd been received. But he didn't leave her under those delusions for long. He quickly made it plain — coarsely plain — why he wanted her. He said she'd been out to vamp him — and, of course, she had — simply because of the family jewels and the chance of a coronet. He told her that if she played with fire, she must be resigned to getting burnt, and asked her why the dickens she thought he'd brought her down there. She told him to behave himself or she'd scream. He cursed her, and told her to get out. She took him quite literally, and got out at once. She packed her bags there and then and told him she was leaving. He just sneered at her, and stormed out of the room.

'Well, Lesley looked up a time-table and found there was a three-coach milk train running to London just after dawn. She caught that, covered in shame because he'd called her a 'so-and-so' vamp, among other things — and, of course, it was partly true.'

'And she didn't see anything suspicious?'

'Not a thing.'

'How about the door she left by? Was it open?'

'Yes. She mentioned that. She said it was

the door to the kitchen garden, and that it was bolted on the inside. She couldn't shut it again once she'd left the place.'

'So it's possible — not probable, but possible — that someone saw her leaving and sneaked in from outside to filch the diamonds? Unless, of course, the thief was a member of the house-party. Did you ask her who else was there?'

'Yes, but she didn't remember. All she'd thought of while she'd been there was how rottenly they'd all treated her. She said there were about five other guests, all of them big noises.'

'But if she hadn't taken the necklace, why didn't she tell you what had made her come home again so quickly?'

'I expect she felt badly about it,' said Sandra. 'You see, I'd told her not to go; told her what I thought of Sorbo. But she'd argued with me, and we'd had rather a nasty quarrel. When she found out that I was right, she didn't like to face me and admit that Sorbo was just another snake, out for what he could get.'

Granger nodded. 'I can understand that, especially as Lesley's young and lovely.

Good grief! Why can't young women realise it's madly dangerous to vamp men?' He paused in thought. 'What did she do when she left the flat after reading the paper?'

'Went straight down to The Sound of Revelry by Night. It seems Popolousilis, the owner, has always had a soft spot for her, and when she told him what a mess she was in, he agreed to give her a hideout until things cooled off. So she dyed her hair and became one of the taxi dancers.'

'Good heavens! Could she have been the kid I danced with? The youngest of them all got horribly alarmed when I mentioned Lesley Lyle.'

Sandra stared at him, then said: 'So the 'snooper' was you? She told me she'd been worried about a man who'd been in last night, and who'd asked her questions about herself. She thought you were a policeman.'

Granger grinned. 'I don't thank her for that. I was under the impression I looked human.'

'So you do,' said Sandra with a smile. 'Very human, Roddy. Lousy told her later that you were a private detective working for the earl. But the biggest shock she had last night was Sorbo's arrival. The viscount knew her at once of course, and nailed her. She thought he was going to be nasty about the necklace, but although he smiled when she claimed she hadn't got it, he told her he was on her side. He even said she was welcome to it. He arranged with Popolousilis to look after her, and said it would be better if she stayed out of sight and didn't even work as a taxi dancer again. After last night she thought so, too; she thought it was a bit funny, Sorbo coming round like that, and asked him if he wasn't still annoyed about the previous night. He said he realised what a cad he'd been, and that he was really very fond of her, and that this would make amends.

'However, in spite of his warnings that she must not stir out in case she was seen, she had to see me. We've always been pretty close, you see. She wrote the note and asked Maudie to take it to me, and you knew the rest.'

'Where is she now?'

'I told her you were helping us, and she said she'd wait until I'd talked things over with you before she gave herself up. She also said she'd telephone Sorbo and Popolousilis, and tell them she intended to do the right thing. I was to go back after I'd seen you, and go with her to the police station. I left her in the hotel room, peroxiding her hair back to its more or less natural shade.'

Granger clambered into his hat and coat. 'I'd like to see her if you don't mind. There are one or two things I want to get straight.'

Sandra nodded, and they left the rooms together. They picked up a taxi, and he glanced at his watch. 'Hmm. Seven-thirty and all's well. Are you sure she'll still be in the hotel?'

'Yes. She said she'd wait there for me. There's a telephone in the lobby that she could use for her calls to Sorbo and Popolousilis.'

The cab groaned across town towards Bayswater Road. The hotel lobby was deserted. But from the bar came the clink of glasses and gusts of laughter. There was the usual stale smell of beer hanging round, and the lobby had that uncomfortable atmosphere of dry leather, spittoons, and furniture polish so common to hotels that are partly public houses. It was an uninspiring place.

Sandra indicated a door on the right and knocked. There was no answer, and she tried again.

'Let me,' Granger said. He knocked more loudly. Still no reply. He stooped and put one eye to the keyhole. He grunted. 'Key's in the lock, and the door's locked. That's queer. It seems there isn't any light on, either. Could she have gone to sleep or not waited? Perhaps she thought better of it and skipped again.'

Sandra thumped at the door. A tall, weedy man in shirt-sleeves and beer-stained whiskers appeared from the end of the lobby. ''Ere, 'ere, wot's orl this 'ere abaht?'

'I want to know about the young lady who took this room,' Granger said. 'Has she checked out?'

'Not with me she ain't ... Martha!'

A short, fat woman with powder-grey hair and red cheeks came hurrying along to his call. He said: ''As the young lass wot took this 'ere room left us yet?'

'Not that I knows of, Bert. Why?'

'These 'ere people wants ter see 'er, I think. Seems they can't get no answer.'

Martha said: 'That's funny. The door was

174

open when the gentleman visited her ten minutes ago. I never saw him go, and I can see along here through the mirror in the bar. I would 'ave seen if he'd gone.'

'What did this man look like?' Granger rapped out.

'Oh, that I couldn't say, sir. I only happened to glance up as he was going in the room. I just spotted the back of his coat, that was all.'

Granger looked at Sandra, whose eyes were wide and troubled. 'Have you a duplicate key for this door?' he asked.

'We have, sir, but we couldn't let you in. It wouldn't be good for business.'

'You needn't worry about business,' he told them urgently. 'I'm a detective. Please open this door at once.'

The woman glanced at her husband, and said: 'Get the key, Bert.'

Bert got the key and came back quickly with it. Granger inserted it into the lock and turned it. The door opened and he went in. By the last fading rays of daylight, he saw the twisted corpse of Lesley Lyle on the old oak floor.

He turned round and closed the door

quickly. 'Sandra, don't come in, dear. Please try to take it bravely. Something has happened to Lesley.'

Sandra gave a little gasp. 'Oh, Roddy — what ...?'

He told her gently: 'She won't have to worry about the stolen necklace, poor kid. Not anymore.'

'Roddy ...'

'Please get the lady a brandy,' he said to Bert. 'See that she's made comfortable.'

He went into the death room again, closing the door behind him. He switched the light on and looked across at the open window. Lesley was lying near the table. She was indeed the woman he had danced with at the nightclub. There was a large purple bruise above her right eye, but this was not the cause of death. Death had come by the silk stocking that was tightly twisted about her throat, and which, with the help of the poker, had been used as a tourniquet to cut off her breathing.

He felt gently for heartbeat and pulse. There were none. Then he stood up again and looked out of the window. There was a short garden with a high wall all round and a half-open back gate at the end of it. Apparently that was the way the killer had gone. He had sneaked in, struck the woman — probably with the poker, then strangled her while she was unconscious.

Granger glanced at her legs — yes, one of her silk stockings had been removed. He sighed, walked to the door, and went out, closing it behind him.

Sandra was dry-eyed, too grief-stricken for tears. She whispered: 'Roddy — oh, Roddy, is she ... really dead?'

He nodded soberly, and her fingers contracted round the stem of her brandy glass. He said: 'Poor kid! There's one consolation, though: she didn't feel anything. Probably didn't even know it was coming. The way I see it, whoever it was who sneaked in, it was most likely a man she knew, and he started talking to her. While her back was turned, he picked up the poker, and when she looked towards him again he struck her down. Then, while she lay senseless, he removed her stocking and strangled her with it.'

'Oh!' shrieked the stout woman. ''Ow 'orrible!'

'It would 'ave to 'appen in our ruddy hotel,' supplied Bert morosely. 'Now we shall 'ave our names in the papers.'

Granger shot him a murderous look. 'If you two had kept your ears open, you might have heard her cry out.'

''Ow the 'eck could we when we was serving in the bar?' said Bert aggrievedly. 'I didn't 'ear nuffink at all, did you, Martha?'

But Martha was in no state to answer. She was having noisy hysterics in one corner, unconscious of the impatient customers in the bar, who were hammering on the counter for some service. Martha was still having hysterics when the police came.

Granger explained as much as he thought would bear explanation, and then asked for formal police permission to take Sandra home. The inspector, a kindly red-faced man, granted it at once, warning them that they'd be needed for questioning the following day.

As they parted, Granger said gently: 'I'm very sorry about all this, Sandra. But the thing to do is to get some action and find the dirty killer who did this. I want you to come over to my place about ten o'clock in the morning, and we'll get down to business. It'll take your mind off everything and give you something to do. Will you come?'

She nodded, not trusting herself to speak. He squeezed her tiny gloved hand, and she murmured: 'I don't know what I'd have done without you, Roddy. I should have gone to pieces.'

As the cab carried him home again, he reviewed the facts. Lesley had seemingly phoned two people: Popolousilis and Sorbo. Could the strangler have been one of these two? Suddenly the whole thing clicked into place, and he knew who had done it and why; saw it all with startling clarity, and cursed himself for not realising it before.

At his flat there was a package waiting for him. It was from Nathan Gideon, and contained three neat files, each typewritten. One was labelled 'Sorbo', one 'Lyle', and the other 'Barter Brand', the notorious fence.

7

Another Glamourous Dame

With unconcealed excitement, Granger carried the files across to his desk, switched on the lamp, and removed the elastic band from each of the boxes. He peered at Nathan's closely typewritten report on Lesley Lyle. It comprised ten quarto sheets and dealt largely with what he already knew.

He laid the woman's file aside, and turned to the one which dealt with Sorbo. This made very interesting reading:

> Sorbo frequents many London nightclubs, but since The Sound of Revelry by Night opened, he seems to favour this establishment, to which gambling rooms are attached. Until recently he was considerably indebted to the owner of the club, having played on credit and lost heavily. The exact sum cannot be ascertained, but it is believed to be somewhere

in the region of twenty thousand pounds, possibly more. This debt, we find, has now been settled. We understand that he is deeply interested in the woman Lesley Lyle (see file one), but of his relationship with her we cannot get full details.

He was seen two weeks ago talking to Barter Brand (see file three), the noted fence, at the above-mentioned club. Recently paid a visit to Rodney Granger, detective, object not known.

Granger grinned. So Nathan's sources of information had even supplied *that* detail! He wondered again exactly how Nathan did it, and again had to give it up. The man's methods were his own secret.

The following pages contained little of value to him, so he turned to file three: Barter Brand. Here Nathan was terse and to the point:

Barter Brand is a darned no-good. He has been raided by the police three times, under search warrant, but each time the raid has failed to reveal anything unusual connected with his premises, and he has threatened court action if there is any repetition of these occurrences. There is no question that Brand is a clever fence, and receives more stolen goods than any other London fence; the question is: where does he hide the swag he receives?

We believe Brand possesses the Marchbrook necklace. Goght Van Beuren, a diamond merchant now in London on a trade visit, is known to have been in communication with Brand, and our investigations have elicited the theory that Brand proposes to dispose of the stolen necklace to him. Brand's assistant, contacted by one of our agents in a public house, revealed that Brand expects a visit from Van Beuren's daughter, Janine, tomorrow morning at eleven. Following this visit, she is to fly immediately to Holland, where her father has already returned today.

The visit to Brand is obviously for the purpose of collecting the necklace purchased by her father. Although this is not certain, we believe it to be true.

Brand has never seen Janine Van Beuren, and as an identifying sign she is to wear green gloves and carry a green handbag. This is all the information our agent was able to obtain from Brand's assistant, who has no idea that Brand is in possession of the stolen necklace, and who thinks the woman's visit is solely for business matters.

There then followed the name and address of the London hotel at which Janine Van Beuren was staying.

'Well,' grunted Granger to himself, 'if *that* little pile of information isn't worth a hundred quid, I don't know what is!'

★   ★   ★

Janine Van Beuren stared lazily from her bed through the east window of the hotel. It was almost nine-thirty, and it was her usual custom to spend the greater part of the morning in bed. This morning, however, sloth must be abandoned. She had business to do — her father's business.

She often helped her father; it was useful to him to have a daughter as pretty and unscrupulous as Janine, and this particular job called for a third person whose interest in diamonds wouldn't render her too conspicuous. No, it wouldn't be the first time she had carried stolen jewels back to her father's shop in Amsterdam, hidden safely in the pouch sewn to the inside of her suspender belt.

She studied herself in the full-length mirror, her firm young body attired in a flimsy nightgown, showed to its best advantage. How many times she had blatantly used her good looks and figure to help her father's business she couldn't remember, but this morning was by far the most important of them all.

She glanced towards the green handbag and gloves she had bought, and which her father had already shown to Brand so that there could be no slip-up. She crossed to the bathroom, turned on the shower, and with a delicious shiver, stood under it.

Stepping out again, she wrapped herself in a bath towel and rubbed herself vigorously. Then she slipped on a transparent negligee and returned to the other room and gaped. The young dark-haired man who was sitting on the bed rose and bowed slightly.

'Good morning, Miss Van Beuren,' he said, smiling at her.

She was not alarmed at the idea of being alone with a strange young man. But although the man was extremely good-looking, and would, at any other moment, have appealed to her immensely, she had no time to waste on him now. She said coldly: 'May I ask who you are, and what you are doing in my bedroom?'

'You may,' he said with a smile. 'I'm here to sell you a handsomely bound set of Dickens for the inclusive price of thirty shillings: with every set sold we give an etching of the author.'

She sat on the bed and said: 'I am trying to get dressed. Will you please stop this nonsense and leave at once?'

He came towards her, still smiling. 'I'm sorry, Miss Van Beuren. I'm afraid I can't leave you for quite a while. My name is Granger, and I'm a detective.'

A glint of fright appeared in her eyes. 'Why have you come here?'

'Surely that's obvious! You know as well as I do that you planned to collect the

Marchbrook necklace this morning.'

She was floored by his bluntness. He went to the door and beckoned to someone outside. A young woman entered.

'All right, Sandra,' he told her, 'pick up the young lady's green gloves and bag. You know what to do with them.'

She nodded, and without even glancing at the petrified woman, helped herself to the bag and gloves. Janine sat and stared, unable to think correctly.

'Now,' said Granger, 'we can sit here and have a pleasant chat — a chat about murder! Or didn't you know that those diamonds have been the cause of one young lady losing her life? Aren't you aware that you can be held as an accessory after the fact?'

Janine didn't try to call for help; she quite believed he was from Scotland Yard, and what was the use of calling for protection against a police officer? Besides, the mention of murder had chilled her. She had not known anything about that at all. 'May — may I go into the bathroom and dress?'

'But certainly.'

'Are you taking me to prison, then?'

'Not for an hour or so. We'll just sit here and have a pleasant chat. Possibly you can tell me a thing or two, eh?'

Sandra said: 'I'll get along now, Roddy.'

'Good luck then — and for heaven's sake be careful!'

She nodded and left.

*   *   *

The assistant at Barter Brand's gave the young lady who had just entered an ingratiating smirk. She was the woman whom the boss had told him to watch for. That was obvious, because she carried the green bag and wore green gloves. But to make sure he said: 'Miss Van Beuren?' The woman nodded pleasantly, and he said: 'Mr. Brand expects you. I'll tell him you're here, miss.'

He vanished behind the showcases, and she waited tensely. The young man returned and said: 'Will you follow me, miss?'

He led her into an inner room. The cadaverous-looking Brand was seated behind a desk, and his eyes noted her bag and gloves. He smiled and said: 'So you've come for the purchase your father made? I'm

Barter Brand.'

He stood up, and she extended her hand, saying: 'How do you do, Mr. Brand? Is it ready?'

He nodded and took a small oblong case from his desk. 'I need hardly warn you to be careful, Miss Van Beuren, eh?'

'I'll take every care, Mr. Brand. You needn't worry.'

She put the package in her handbag, and he went on: 'Tell your father I'll be pleased to do business with him again at some later date. He'll find the diamonds well worth the trouble, my dear.'

She nodded, and he escorted her to the door. As they passed the show cases, the corner of one of them hooked against the small hat she was wearing and pulled it from her head.

The assistant obligingly retrieved it from the floor, and Sandra hastily put it on and went out.

'A charming young woman,' said Brand to the young man. 'Comes of an excellent family.'

The assistant, however, was looking rather puzzled. 'There's one funny thing, sir,' he said. 'If her name's Van Beuren, why does she have the name Sandra Lyle inside her hat?'

'*What?*' bawled Brand.

'In her hat, sir — on a tag. I spotted it when I picked the hat up.'

'*Good grief!*' exploded Brand. '*Quick* — Phillips — follow that woman, and don't let her out of your sight. When she's got wherever she's going, telephone me instantly. I'll wait here for your call.'

★ ★ ★

For the tenth time Janine Van Beuren said: 'I don't know how Mr. Brand got the diamonds. I don't know anything about it. I only did what Father told me.'

'Okay,' Granger said. 'If you won't talk turkey now, maybe we can get it out of you at police headquarters.'

'You'll be lucky. Why should I talk? What good would it do me?'

'Just this,' rapped Granger. 'I'd give you a chance to get away before I put the police on to you.'

'But — but you're a policeman, aren't

you?'

He grinned and said: 'No. Private detective.'

She came closer to him. 'Is that true? You'd let me go if I told you what I know?'

'If the information was worth it. Actually, all I want you to do is confirm something I already suspect. Namely, that the person who stole the Marchbrook necklace was none other than Lord Sorbo! Is that right?'

'Yes, that's right. It was all planned a month ago. Lord Sorbo was to steal the necklace and turn it over to Brand. Brand was to pay twenty-five thousand for it, and Father was buying it back from him for thirty-five thousand. That's why we came over here.'

'I see. And the woman — Lesley Lyle?'

'That was Sorbo's idea. He planned to throw the blame on her. He knew very well his parents would insult her if he took her home with him and he planned to make things worse by insulting her himself in the middle of the night. He knew the type she was, and knew she'd leave at once rather than put up with that. And that's just what happened. Then he got frightened of her being taken by the police. He thought that once she was in their hands, they might find out too much. When he found out she was in hiding, he encouraged her to stay that way.'

'Was there anyone else besides Brand, Sorbo, your father, and you in this thing?'

'No one. The idea was Sorbo's at first, and he contacted Brand. Brand contacted Father, and Father expressed an avid interest in the Marchbrook necklace. He once tried to buy it openly. Sorbo wanted money to pay his debts because Popolousilis was threatening to tackle his father. That's how it all happened. I didn't — didn't know anything about the murder.'

She broke off as the door opened and Sandra walked in. Granger said: 'Get it?'

She nodded, and patted her bag. Granger turned to Janine. 'I always did have a soft spot for a pretty face. I'm giving you an hour to get to Croydon and make that plane. Then I'm putting the police on your track.'

'Thank you, Mr. Granger.' She started throwing her things haphazardly into her bag. Then she snapped it shut, turned suddenly, and presented a small revolver at Granger, who had just taken the diamond case from Sandra. She snapped: 'Thank you, Mr. Granger. I'll take those!'

He knew by the glint in her eye she meant business. He snapped the case shut and handed it to her. '*Au revoir*, Miss Van Beuren!' he said. She took the key from the lock, let herself out, and locked the door behind her.

8

Ladies Are Dangerous

When Janine Van Beuren had gone, Sandra looked at Granger with wide eyes. 'Aren't you going to follow her?'

'No. She won't be fool enough to go to Croydon. The main thing now is to get Sorbo. Sorbo was the one who killed Lesley.'

'Sorbo?'

'None other. Wasn't it obvious? We'll see he swings for it. Let's go.'

He led her towards the door which Janine had locked on the outside. He took a small leather pouch from his pocket, extracted a curved piece of metal, fitted it to the lock and turned it. 'Simple locks they have here. A burglar's paradise! Come on.'

They walked quickly out into the passage. Then Brand, who had just arrived and had had time only to send away his assistant, presented a revolver at them and said: 'Back into that room, please.'

'Mercy! Another termite!' exclaimed Granger. 'Do as he says, Sandra. It isn't a lollipop he's holding.'

They went backwards, keeping their eyes on Brand, who followed them closely, saying: 'Now I'll take the diamonds; and, incidentally, you can tell me everything you know.'

'You can't take the diamonds,' Granger told him. 'Janine Van Beuren has already left with them.'

'Don't lie,' Brand snapped. He glared at Sandra. 'This woman came to my shop for them. She took them.'

'You're welcome to search us if you insist, but I give you my word Miss Van Beuren has them.'

'Then — then there's no evidence against — against me?' stammered Brand, hardly able to believe his good luck.

'Apparently not.'

For a moment Brand looked blank; then he went on: 'You actually say Miss Van Beuren is at this moment in possession of the gems?'

'Exactly.'

'She — she's taking them to her father?' he asked.

'I imagine so — if she can get them out of the country.'

Brand threw back his head and unexpectedly laughed. That was his undoing. Granger had shown no sign of hostility since his entrance, and the fence had become careless. Granger had waited for this moment, and the next thing that Brand knew was the thud of a bony fist crashing into his mouth, callously cutting short his chuckles. He went backwards, revolver spinning futilely across the room. He lay where he fell, breathing hard, eyes closed, a trickle of blood running down his chin.

Granger waited patiently for him to come round. At last Brand's eyes flickered, and Granger hauled him into the bathroom. To Sandra he said: 'Wait here, dear. And I wouldn't listen too closely if I were you. What's going to happen may make nasty hearing.' Then he shut the bathroom door behind him.

Sandra sat and waited, hands clenched. From the bathroom came the thud of heavy blows, and the sound of hard fists battering soft flesh. One or two gasping cries sidled beneath the door, and Sandra shuddered.

Once there was a thin scream. Then the sound of fighting ceased, and she heard Brand cry: 'No more I'll — I'll tell you everything.'

His voice trailed away into a continuous murmur, and this went on for ten minutes. Then the door opened and Granger lugged out the fence. His face was badly bruised and blood-smeared, both his eyes were closed tightly, and two front teeth were missing. His lips were cut and broken, and his hair hung over his blackened eyes. Granger, however, had sustained nothing worse than a split cheek.

He hauled Brand to the bed and tied him up with the sheets. He said: 'He talked — confirmed all that Janine said. And also the fact that Sorbo murdered your sister. It seems she telephoned the nightclub to tell Popolousilis she meant to give herself up. Sorbo was there, and took the call. She told him. He probably said he'd like to see her first, and went up and murdered her. I expect he was afraid that if the police got her, they'd find out too much. Popolousilis wasn't in on the theft at all; he only sheltered Lesley because he felt some affection for her.'

'Then we must get hold of Sorbo?'

'Yes. Brand tells me he'll probably be at the The Sound of Revelry by Night. I think he has some sort of understanding with Lady Lossa. We'll get along there now; we can leave Brand locked in here until we get the police.'

Leaving Brand firmly tied, they left the room again. The fence watched them from one half-closed eye, then lay back on the bed with a groan as Granger locked the door with his master key.

★   ★   ★

'What on earth do you carry *this* for?' said Lady Lossa, hauling a gun from Lord Sorbo's pocket.

Sorbo snapped: 'Give me that. Never mind why I carry it. It's none of your business.'

She looked at him shrewdly. 'Are you in trouble, darling?'

'It isn't your affair if I am. Shut up!'

'Oh, don't be peevish. I assure you I'm not interested in what you do, but I do object to having a surly fool making himself at home in my rooms.'

Sorbo tried to curb his bad temper. 'Sorry. I didn't mean to be boorish. I value your friendship, Lossa. We're both from the same set, and we're both outcasts from it. It's a good job we have each other to turn to.'

'You *must* be worried,' she said. 'I've never heard you talk like that before. Usually you think you're too smart for your own kind.'

He grunted and accepted the whisky she offered him. When he'd drained it, he pulled her down on the arm of the chair beside him and said: 'I like you because you never talk of marriage. Why can't other women be like that?'

Lady Lossa gave him a wise, sophisticated smile. 'Why? I suppose because other women have so much to lose. If I had anything to lose, I expect I'd be like other women. But I haven't.'

There was a sudden knock on the door and a voice called: 'It's me — Popolousilis. There's a telephone call for Lord Sorbo.'

'All right. Let him in, Lossa.'

Lousy said: 'The call's from Brand. He

says they've found out everything — who murdered the woman, and who stole the necklace, and they're coming for you.'

Sorbo went ash-grey. He gasped: 'Heaven help me!'

Lousy said: 'You don't want to count on *that* too much.'

Sorbo stood up. His eyes were desperate as he gazed wildly at Lousy and Lady Lossa. He stammered: 'You two — you'll have to help me.'

'Like blazes I will,' said Lady Lossa. 'I always knew you were several varieties of a swine, but I never thought you'd kill!'

'If I'd known you were the one who strangled Lesley Lyle,' said Lousy, 'I'd have helped you all right. I'd have killed you with my own hands. Now I don't need to. Come in, Mr. Granger.'

Sorbo recoiled as Granger walked in, followed by Sandra Lyle. Granger said: 'I think we've enough witnesses to pin the killing where it belongs. Better not make too much fuss, Sorbo.'

'Look out,' said Lossa suddenly. 'He's got a —'

She was too late; Sorbo's left arm

clamped suddenly around her throat and over her chest, and he pulled her to him. Simultaneously, his right hand streaked to his pocket for his gun, and he levelled it at the three in the doorway. 'Don't try to draw, Granger. If you do, the first to die will be your lady-friend.'

The three didn't move. 'Get away from that door,' Sorbo said. 'Go towards the other room. Go on.'

He couldn't see the look Lady Lossa gave Granger; he had no idea that her right hand was coming up stealthily towards the arm he had about her neck.

Granger and his party had started to move; his attention was fixed on them, looking for false moves — and then Lady Lossa acted!

Her right hand grasped his wrist, her body curved; he sailed over her head with a yelp of fear and landed sprawling in front of her. He came to his feet, snarling, just in time to receive the jaw-shattering punch which Granger had led.

★　★　★

200

'Don't mention it,' said Lady Lossa modestly some weeks later, when Granger complimented her on her handling of Sorbo. 'I learned a trick or two from a handsome young man I once knew — a judo expert. You have to be able to look after yourself when you're a paid escort, as I told you once before. Oh, and by the way, thanks awfully for the share in the earl's fee. I can use that five hundred.'

'Don't mention *that* either,' said Granger with a smile. 'You deserved it. It was rather rough luck the earl having to pay up for the capture of his own flesh and blood — if you could call Sorbo flesh and blood; but after all, if you have a son like that, it's just as well to get rid of him. I believe he put up a rotten show when they dragged him to the scaffold. He was yellow all through.'

Lady Lossa shuddered. 'Well, I'll push along. I can see by the way Sandra's looking at us that she wants to get you alone.'

She left the office. Sandra at once came round and parked herself on Granger's knee. She said: 'I can't understand why the earl paid you ten thousand when he didn't get his diamonds back.'

'But he did,' said Granger. 'Didn't you know that?'

She looked puzzled. 'How could he? Didn't Janine Van Beuren escape with them?'

'No. Why do you think I let her take those diamonds so calmly when she held us up? I'll tell you — simply because the moment I saw them, I knew they were fakes! Barter Brand was double-crossing Goght Van Beuren, and he knew the man wouldn't have any comeback since the stuff was stolen. He was sending him paste replicas. The real stones were in his safe, under the carpet in his shop. He told me that when I beat him up. The police found them on my information. That's why the earl paid my *full fee*, darling.'

'Then — then Janine has taken a collection of fakes back to her father?' He nodded, and the humour of it suddenly struck her. Sandra laughed until his lips cut off her laughter.

Miss Green popped her head round the office door and said: 'Will you receipt this …? My, my! Excuse me!' She withdrew. A moment passed. Her head popped in again. She said scathingly: '*You wolf you!*'

Granger paused from his labours for a moment to wink at her and say: 'Not this time, Miss Green. Not this time!'

Other titles in the
Linford Mystery Library:

THE EMERALD CAT KILLER

Richard A. Lupoff

A valuable cache of stolen comic books originally brought insurance investigator Hobart Lindsey and police officer Marvia Plum together. Their tumultuous relationship endured for seven years, then ended as Plum abandoned her career to return to the arms of an old flame, while Lindsey's duties carried him thousands of miles away. Now, after many years apart, the two are thrown together again by a series of crimes, beginning with the murder of an author of lurid private-eye paperback novels and the theft of his computer, containing his last unpublished book . . .

ANGELS OF DEATH

Edmund Glasby

A private investigator uncovers more than he bargained for when he looks into the apparent suicide of an accountant . . . What secrets are hiding inside the sinister house on the coast of Ireland that Martin O'Connell has inherited from his eccentric uncle . . . ? A hitherto unknown path appears in the remote Appalachians, leading Harvey Peterson deep into the forest — and a fateful encounter . . . And an Indian prince invites an eclectic group of guests to his palace to view his unique menagerie — with unintended consequences . . . Four tales of mystery and murder.

TERROR STALKS BY NIGHT

Norman Firth

In *Terror Stalks by Night*, when the mutilated corpse of old Lucille Rivers is found lying in her decrepit mansion, Rivers End, the damage appears to be the work of the razor-sharp claw of some monstrous animal. One week later, the remaining members of the Rivers family gather at Rivers End to listen to the reading of the will — but one by one they are systematically slaughtered! While in *Phantom of Charnel House*, a grisly apparition prowls the newly built Charnel Estate, bringing hideous death to all it encounters!

WHERE BLOOD RUNS DEEP

Edmund Glasby

Private investigator Patrick Haskell is hired by a concerned father to follow up the disappearance of his son. The young man, an avid historian, was researching the phenomenon of 'ghost villages' — abandoned communities, one of which, Witherych, is rumoured to lie close to the isolated, squalid settlement of Marshwood. What starts as a routine investigation becomes anything but as his covert inquiries amongst the xenophobic inhabitants are met with suspicion and hostility. Haskell becomes increasingly convinced that Marshwood harbours a sinister secret . . .